CW00339444

Red Silver!

When Lon Burton rode into Virginia City he knew it was the town for him. Not for nothing was it called Silver City for it had more riches – and more sin – than any other place in the West and that was just what Lon sought. Of course that wasn't his real name and his current image belied his gunfighter past. Even so, he was a hell-raiser as the gambling joints and saloons soon found out.

Behind all this, though, was a more serious side and Lon soon found himself badly beaten up and almost fatally wounded. He was now working for the good of Virginia City and, henceforth, would be the target of every gunslinger.

The only question was: could he still palm his guns more quickly and shoot more accurately than almost any man around?

Red Silver!

Charlie Potts

A Black Horse Western

ROBERT HALE · LONDON

ISBN 0 7090 7273 2

Robert Hale Limited
Clerkenwell House
Clerkenwell Green
London EC1R OHT

Typeset by
Derek Doyle & Associates, Liverpool.
Printed and bound in Great Britain by
Antony Rowe Limited, Wiltshire

ONE

As soon as Lon Burton rode into Virginia City on that raw blustering Saturday night he knew it was the town for him.

The main drag was all lights and noise and movement, and at the top of it the black mountain brooded like some dark presence casting a spell over it all.

It cast a spell over Lon.

'Silver City' they called it. More riches – and more sin – here right now than in any other place in the West. There was an atmosphere of glittering recklessness over the place which fired Lon Burton's blood as he dismounted from his horse outside a honky-tonk.

He tied the reins to the hitching-rack and mounted the three board steps to the sidewalk. Then he turned on his heels and looked out into the street. Its surface consisted of hard-baked mud rutted deeply by cartwheels and pitted by holes. Even as Lon watched, on the other side of the street a horse stumbled and rolled over on its side. Its rider, a big fellow in a top-heavy wide-awake, was thrown clear but lashed out at the horse with a booted foot.

Lon felt his jaw-muscles tighten. His hand clutched his belt, convulsively, near the butt of his low-slung gun. Out of the corner of his eye he saw two men leaning against the hitching-rack a few yards away, watching him. The air was suddenly tense.

He relaxed as the horse got to its feet, and the big fellow mounted. A carriage and pair rumbled and clattered up the street and drew up in a cloud of dust which hung in the air, mixing with the pungent dust of the silver mines and the stamping mills.

A girl had been driving the open carriage. She tossed the reins to the bovine-looking man beside her and, lifting her voluminous skirts a little, got down from the box. One of the men against the hitching-rack whistled shrilly between his teeth.

The girl lifted her head as she mounted the steps, tripping daintily in her long red cloak. Her black hair swept down to her shoulders and had jewels in it. On the fingers that held the skirt above tiny shoes and trim ankles there were jewelled rings. Her black eyes settled on Lon Burton's face for a moment then passed on. They were like glittering gems too. With them he had the impression of a dark arrogant beautiful face, full red lips which shone moistly, glittering drops dangling from small white ears. Then she passed through into the honky-tonk. Not a place for women, he thought. Not good women anyway.

Still, she looked like she could take care of herself. If she wanted to take care of herself.

He was turning to follow in her wake when a gangling white-faced youth with a curiously startled expression ran along the boardwalk and plucked at his arm.

'Can I look after your hoss, mister?' he said in a high whining voice. 'I'll take him down the stables an' feed him an' bed him down . . . .'

The light from the window shone on the white face as Lon looked into it, and he realized the startled expression was caused by the fact that the kid had no lids to his eyes and no eyebrows either. The eyes were shifty and appealing. The whole effect was horrible, and Lon felt a spasm of pity.

He was opening his mouth to speak when bootheels thudded behind him. He half turned, catlike, on his high-heeled boots.

A man went past him. A gruff voice said: 'Mosey along, Shiner,' and the boy turned and scuttled away into the shadows. Lon found himself facing one of the men who had been leaning against the hitching-rack. He could feel the presence of the other one behind him.

The first one was big and florid-faced. He said: 'Sorry to butt in, suh. If you let thet kid have yuh boss it's likely you'd never see him again.' His pouched little eyes flickered up and down Lon's lean body. 'He takes every stranger f'r a tenderfoot. One o' these days he'll get his hide perforated for keeps.' His tone, his eyes, his manner conveyed the fact that *he* did not take Lon for a tenderfoot.

The other man moved to Lon's side. He was squat and heavy. They were too close – Lon felt hemmed in by them. He stepped back a little – casually. He said 'The kid seemed harmless enough.'

'Oh, he's harmless awlright,' said the squat man. 'Only like lots o' folk in this burg he ain't got no respeck for other folks's property.'

7

The big man said: 'If you want to stable your hoss there's a place around the back o' The Venus.' He indicated the establishment before which they stood and which went by the grandiose appellation of The Venus Bar.

'He's only jest rode in.' said the squat man. 'Mebbe he'd like a drink first. How about it, stranger? I'm Jed Crample an' this big galoot yere is my pard, Oakie Jones. Welcome to Washoe.'

'I guess I do need a drink,' said Lon. *Welcome to Washoe*, the magic name. The silver country. The land of the get-rich-quick, of vice and ballyhoo, of bad women and forgotten men. Here he was in the middle of it at last. The hub of the wheel. *Welcome to Washoe*. Was that welcome genuine or was it as false as the look of the place, the sound of the place, the brittle hardness of the place, which intrigued him so much? It intrigued him because he was a little like that himself, though he found it hard to admit the fact.

He followed the two men into The Venus and was met by a blast of hot smoky air, laden with the smell of liquor and sweating human flesh and cigarette-smoke and scent. The noise, which heard outside had been part of the town, part of all the rest of the cacophony of sound out there, was now a living presence which seemed to swirl around him, enfold him, draw him to it like the warm arms of a scented woman. It was made up of the clankety beat of a barrel-house piano, the wheezy squeal of a concertina, the twang of a guitar, the tortured notes of a battered cornet. And the drunken singing of men, the squeals and laughter of women, the thumping of feet and the clapping of hands, the babble of loud-mouthed voices,

8

the accents of almost every nationality under the sun, men from the mines and the mills, teamsters, gamblers, gunmen, pimps, confidence men, business men – all part of the stinking melting pot that was 'Washoe'.

He followed his newfound friends to the bar, the huge Oakie pushing his way through the press like a steam-tug through sluggish waters, being greeted here and there, and slapped on the shoulders, as he did so.

Men moved aside at the bar, leaving a place for Oakie and his two pards. The big florrid-faced man said:

'What'll yuh have, Mister—'

There was a lilt in his voice at the end, a note held.

'Call me Hank,' said Lon Burton. 'Hank Blundell's the name. I'll have a large rye.'

'Shore thing, Hank.' Oakie raised his voice. 'Four big ones, Jamie.'

'Yes, suh, Mr Jones,' said the oily-faced barman.

He served their order in double-quick time. Oakie threw a bill on the bar with a magnanimous gesture. Lon sized him up. His black broadcloth was creased and spotty through ill-use, but good stuff. His coat flew open and there was an ornamental belt across his broad belly but no signs of a gun. But Lon had already nudged the bulge at his side and knew that he carried a heavy piece of hardware in a shoulder-holster. Although he favoured the old-fashioned way himself he had heard that this new rig, on a good man, was the fastest drawing ever and was favoured by gamblers, bruisers and professional gunmen in this part of the country. Oakie Jones did not seem to fit into any of these categories. Maybe he was carrying a gun for

9

'protection' same as everybody else.

His pardner Jed Crample looked like a cowhand or a teamster. With his dusty boots almost knee-high, his washed-out check shirt, and greasy leather vest, his heavy cartridge-studded belt and walnut-handled forty-eight. A .48 was kind of a heavy gun for a quick draw, but Jed, with his low-browed face, monkey-build and long arms, looked strong enough to handle it.

Lon wondered why these two ill-assorted examples of humanity had singled him out for their special attention. Maybe they ran a boarding-house or a gambling joint and were soliciting for custom, maybe they were pimping for some fat madam with a bevy of girls . . . . Hell, maybe he was being over-suspicious as usual, maybe, like they said, they were just being friendly. *Welcome to Washoe.*

He half-emptied his glass and put it back on the bar. He said: 'That kid who stopped me outside – what's his game?'

It was the omnipotent Oakie who answered. 'Shiner's kind of a mascot around here. When he was a kid him an' his big sister and his maw and paw were caught by Injuns. He was jest getting old enough to understand things. They tied him to a tree and made him watch while they got to work on his folks. You can imagine what they did to the women before they finally finished them off. They roasted the old man over a slow fire an' cut slices off him with their knives until he was dead. The kid watched it all. After it was all finished they started on him. They got to work on him with their knives . . . .'

'Those eyes of his,' said Lon. 'I figured that was Injun work.'

'That ain't nuthin',' said Jed suddenly. 'You oughta see his body. They tattooed the pore crittur.'

Then Oakie went on: 'It seems that this Injun band was led by a renegade who called himself White Fox. I guess he thought it'd be funny to let the kid go – so he'd be a living example of the red man's hate for the white. So he made his bucks let him loose.'

'You talk real purty, friend,' said Lon Burton.

Oakie grinned. 'I ain't no school-teacher,' he said. 'But I've been places an' I've read things.'

'Oakie's a scholar,' said Jed.

Here was another strange facet to the big man's character. Lon Burton listened intently as Oakie went on. 'The kid wandered this way an' was picked up by ol' Pop, who found the first silver-mine in this territory. The mine's long since petered out an' Pop's dead an' gone. Pop helped build this town an' he brought up his half-crazy boy along with it. When Pop died the town kind of adopted the kid. Pop called him jest "Boy", but most everybody calls him 'Shiner', the way he's so eager-like an' his eyes shine.'

'I noticed that.'

'There ain't no harm in 'Shiner' 'cept he's allus stealin'. He only steals off'n strangers who come in – particularly if he thinks they're tenderfeet. Right now he seems to have a craze for hosses. What he does with 'em nobody seems to know – unless he sells 'em for work in the mine. Though what he does with the money – if he gets any – is hard to know too – he can get all he wants in this town without paying for it. Some folks think it lucky to touch his lidless eyes – they'll pay him to sit by 'em when they're gambling.

11

Some o' the sharpshooters hate him like pizen, but they dassent do nuthin' about it, him bein' simple-like an' having all the older townsfolk to look out for him.'

'He didn't sound simple to me,' said Lon Burton.

'No, that's the queer part about it. He can talk almost like a normal man when he wants to. Now f'rinstance, Mister – er – Hank. It was Hank wasn't it?' Oakie paused.

'Yeh, Hank's the name.'

'Yeh, wal, say f'rinstance, Hank, that Shiner had taken your hoss. You look like a riding-man to me, an' I guess you're kinda fond of your hoss. If Shiner took your hoss an' you didn't see it again you'd be mighty peeved at Shiner wouldn't yuh?'

'I guess so.'

'An' when you saw him again you'd want to take it out of his hide wouldn't yuh?'

'I guess so.'

'Wal, that'd be when Shiner 'ud act simple. He wouldn't remember you or your hoss an' you'd be in bad with everybody for picking on a pore dumb crittur who ain't got the sense to defend himself. I seed a man tarred an' feathered an' run outa town on a rail on'y last week because he mistreated Shiner. He claimed Shiner stole his saddle.'

'Did he?'

Oakie shrugged. 'Who can tell.' Then he went on reflectively: 'Funny thing about Shiner is the way he looks into strangers' faces. Folks around here say he's lookin' for the renegade who killed his maw and paw an' his sister, an' if he found the renegade he'd kill him – then he wouldn't be simple any more, he'd be just like you an' me.'

12

'It was a long time ago wasn't it, when that happened?'

'Yep, a helluva long time. There ain't bin no wild Injuns around here in ages. Seems like White Fox an' his merry men plumb vanished when folks started finding silver around here an' opening mines, an' Washoe was born. But maybe that renegade's face is imprinted on the boy's memory, maybe that's the only thing he can remember, maybe he's tellin' the truth when he says he don't remember about the things he's supposed to've stolen, but maybe he'll remember that dirty renegade right off as soon as he sees him again.'

'That's a mighty interesting story, Oakie,' said Lon Burton. 'I almost wish I had let the boy have my hoss jest to see what would happen. He's just a nag I picked up back aways. My old hosss broke a leg an' I had to shoot him.'

'My, that's a pity, Hank,' said the apish Jed. Then, looking past him Lon Burton saw the girl once more.

She had taken off her red cloak and wore a tight-fitting black dress of a satin stuff which had a glittering sheen beneath the lights. Her black hair was coiled on top of her head in an elaborate pile which seemed to be clipped up by a handful of stars. The dress was very low-cut and revealed a creamy expanse of bosom. She still had red on her: at her breast, at her shoulder, at her hip; blood-red flowers.

Lon watched her wend her way through the crowd, her black eyes bold yet somehow disdainful. He stiffened as he saw a burly miner paw at her then stagger away with a ludicrous expression of anguish on his face. Lon had not seen the girl raise her hands. He

13

figured she must have kicked the fellow.

Her progress stopped when she was beside a shirt-sleeved, eye-shaded dealer at a faro layout. The dealer was standing against the wall on a small box so that he was a little above the players at his table and could see what was going on better. When he stepped down the watching man realized how short he was. He really needed the box. The girl was a mite taller when she took the dealer's place. She took the green eyeshade too and put the elastic loop over her own head. It gave her a mysterious look as she brooded over the table. Even from where he was Lon heard her clear, rather brassy voice say: 'Place your bets, gentlemen.'

The shirt-sleeved dealer took his place as her assistant on the right-hand and after a bit of surreptitious manoeuvring Lon spotted the assistant on the left, a ruffish-looking young man in black.

TWO

By this time Oakie was following the direction of Lon's gaze and he said:

'That's Lulu Sanclaire, The Venus's ace dealer. She's a hell-cat.'

'Are there many female dealers in this town?'

'There's Phoebe an' Ella down at Croner's place, but they ain't much. They both drink too much. They let the boys paw 'em an' start fights. It spoils the game.' Oakie's voice was almost melancholy.

Lon, pretending to lose interest, turned back to the bar. 'Set 'em up again, pardner,' he said.

Jamie, the barman, obeyed with alacrity. Lon figured it was not for his benefit but for Oakie's. He wondered where exactly the big fellow stood in this town. Not at the bottom evidently.

The three of them leaned with their elbows on the bar and settled down to some serious drinking. Lon figured that maybe if Oakie wanted to tell him something he could wait.

He was looking through the huge ornate mirror in front of him when he saw the doors open and the little man in the grey broadcloth and gaudily flowered vest

15

come into the place. And the three men with him, hard faces, hard eyes, arms brushing gun-butts – professionals. He saw Oakie's face, beside his own, change a little. Then the expression was gone, and Oakie was lifting his glass and finishing his liquor. But Lon noticed that other men were turning and looking at the little man and that the place suddenly did not seem quite so rowdy. A table cleared miraculously in the centre of the joint and the little man and his retinue sat down. Liquor was produced, three bottles of the best: it was brought to the table by three girls, and the little man smiled at them and pinched their cheeks. But all the time his little black-button eyes were never still, they were looking around the room, and everywhere that they looked the hard eyes of the gunmen looked too. The four pairs of eyes passed over the reflection of Lon Burton's face in the mirror, and he knew that one pair of them had recognized him but given no sign – except to him who knew them so well.

After that the four men settled down to their drinking. The little man was 'somebody' in Virginia City. He was liked maybe – or feared – and hated most probably; or why the gunmen? Lon Burton marvelled at the vanity of the man who desired a table in the middle of the room where he could be shot at from every side, yet hired gunmen to guard against that very eventuality.

Lon Burton's eyes were shifty then. He bet he could plug the little man if he wanted to – and get away with it! From up there on the balcony he could do it. Or from the musicians' dais, which had a trap behind it leading through the bar to a little back door. Or from that dealer's position over by the window, as a last resort, and crash through the window afterwards. If the little man was

16

killed what would be the town's reaction? Would they be glad or would they be sorry? Maybe half-and-half, maybe a little more on one side than the other. But which side?

Out of the corner of his mouth Oakie Jones said: 'That's Hiram Vanberger. He owns the biggest mine in the territory. Folks say he's aimin' to be Virginia City's first mayor. I make him out a crook.'

'He seems popular.'

'Yeh, men like him are allus popular – when they're on top. He's got plenty o' lickspittlers on his payroll – an' plenty o' lickspittlers who'd like to be.'

'That's the way o' things,' said Lon. He shrugged. 'Me, I think I'll go buck the tiger.'

He turned. Oakie grinned. 'I figured you'd want to do that sooner or later, Hank,' he said. 'I figure I know which table you aim to place your bets at too.'

The three of them wended their way through the throng and reached the outskirts of the ring around Lulu Sanclaire's layout.

'The boys sure like to play that table,' said Oakie. 'I guess it's the nearest most of 'em get to Lulu.'

The three of them waited a bit, saw their chance and wormed their way in. They placed their bets. Lon knew that the girl must be watching all the players from beneath the eye-shade, but he could not tell when her eyes were on him. He looked at her boldly, feasted his eyes on her. Lush was the word to describe her. Lush. And maybe dangerous.

He watched her long white fingers, loaded with rings which looked like the real thing, manipulating the cards from the dealing-box on the table in front of her. Her movements were as sure and as smooth as

17

any big shot gambler he had ever seen at work. She was like a beautiful machine.

'Place your bets, gentlemen,' she said. In that clear voice with the little rasping undertone. 'The sky's the limit.'

That was the call that every good gambler likes to hear, and Lon Burton was no exception to the rule. Together with Jed and Oakie he laid his bets. His and Oakie's were the highest on the table.

Lulu began to draw the cards from the 'box' – left, right – left, right. She concentrated fully on what she was doing and worked with the precision of a machine. Stakes mounted, and everything seemed to be on the side of the bank. The players watched avidly, some of them with expressionless faces, only their eyes giving them away to the seasoned professionals on the other side of the table.

Lon Burton was a poker face. He glanced sideways at Oakie. *His* face was like red, polished rock, his paunced eyes, which had been so shifty before, were still and empty. Lon figured the big fellow would be a hard customer to buck any time. What exactly *was* his 'game'?

Lulu's left-hand assistant, the young man in black, had a miniature layout before him, a tiny replica of the one before the players: thirteen cards, all spades, glued onto a square of shiny black oilcloth. The assistant moved his pointer along on his miniature layout to indicate the cards as they were being dealt, and the players checked on the big one.

The right-hand assistant, who had been dealing before the girl turned up, paid and collected the bets and kept a watchful eye on the players.

18

He was sleek and tubby and had a thin black moustache and sideburns. His eyes were like bottle-green marbles. They seemed to roll in their sockets – none of the players were free from their baleful scrutiny.

The first game finished and the 'bank' seemed to have the inside edge. Players drifted away and others took their places. Oakie, Jed and Lon Burton (alias Hank Blundell) stayed put. Oakie and Lon let themselves go again, but Jed seemed to be a 'piker'. He was obviously only staying put because his two pards were. His stake was pitifully small.

Lulu shuffled the pack, cut the cards and placed them face upwards in the open-topped dealing box. The top, exposed, card known as 'dead' and not counting in play, was the six of hearts.

Lulu began to draw the cards through the slit in the box, placing them to the left and to the right, the winning cards nearest to the players and the others close to her hand. She was fast and her arms worked like well-oiled levers. Lon Burton had played faro in 'hells' and backrooms all over the States, but he figured he had never come across a dealer quite so slick as this girl. He knew faro too well to have faith in any layout, but if this one was 'rigged' he was hard put to discover how. He knew it was taken for granted by many players that every 'tiger' layout was rigged in some way or another, but sometimes a dealer went too far, tried to cut his losses to a bare minimum by using trimmed, sanded, or marked cards. Some of them used crooked dealing-boxes. Smart folks were inventing new and more complicated ones all the time.

The one Lulu was using was the old type made of metal with an open top, a slit for dealing and a spring to release a new card as the one above it was dealt. These kind were the fairest in use, and if this one was rigged at all Lon was sure it was a new innovation that he had not seen before – and he thought he had seen them all. Maybe the cards were fixed somehow or maybe, after years, he had discovered that rarity, the 'square' faro layout.

The bank was not doing so well this time, though none of the three at the dealer's side of the table revealed by any change of expression that they were aware of the fact. Nevertheless, Lon Burton still did not like the look of the right-hand assistant who paid and collected with mechanical motions, but whose green glassy eyes watched every movement the other side made.

His companion the other side, who manipulated the 'case-keeper' and from time to time intoned the numbers, was whiplike and nonchalant. He looked harmless but was the type who could be mighty fast if need be. Between them the girl was like a dark Sphinx.

The press around the table was getting thicker as more lookers-on joined the ranks. This layout was by far the most popular in the place. Lon Burton figured the folks came more to watch Lulu than the game. She was certainly a sight for sore eyes.

The noise and the smell and the jostling people whirled away in waves from the circle around the table. The band played 'Turkey in the Straw' and a boot-thumping, nasally-barking singer tried to get a dance going. In some measure he succeeded, although there was not much room for actual dancing, as burly miners, teamsters and saddle-tramps jostled intimately with squealing percentage-girls.

The place was getting fuller every minute, the

greater press of folks being around Lulu's layout, while the crowd washed away a little from the centre table at which sat young-old wizened Hiram Vanberger and his three gun-toters.

The jousting, the gaming and the festivities were at their height when other, unforeseen, things began to happen.

A drunken man lurched as he was passing the table of Vanberger and his retinue. He crashed into the little man and almost knocked him from his chair – then sprawled full-length on the floor.

He was rising when one of Vanberger's men stood over him and with calculated brutality kicked him full in the face. The man groaned and fell flat once more, blood pouring from a smashed nose.

Somewhere in the crowd somebody cried out in indignation. The other two gunmen rose and looked around the room. Vanberger sat immobile, sipping daintily at a glass of the finest Scotch whisky that money could buy. Voices died to a murmur. The band played on raucously.

'Get this mangy polecat out of here,' bawled one of the gunmen. 'He's making a mess.'

Two white-aproned bruisers came across, heaved the groaning drunk to his feet and propelled him through the doors.

At the faro layout Lulu continued to deal, but many of the players turned to see what was going on, craning their necks in order not to miss anything.

Lon Burton was too seasoned a gambler to follow their example. He kept his eyes on the layout.

It was then he saw the right-hand dealer's hand

21

slide along the under rim of the table and a flicker of white there. Lulu's white fingers were reaching out to meet the card when Lon barked:

'Hold it there!'

The green-eyed man tried to palm the card in his left hand. His other one dropped.

Lon Burton's draw was as smooth as grease. 'Let's see those hands – both of 'em !'

The man raised them slowly. Lulu was motionless, but the young man at her left made a sudden movement. Then he froze as another voice said: 'All right, son.'

Out of the corner of his eye Lon saw that Oakie had a gun in his hand too.

He moved around the table and picked up the card the 'looker-out' had dropped on the floor.

'There's your ace in the hole, pardner,' he said. He tossed it face upwards on the shiny oilcloth.

The faro layout became the centre of all eyes. Lulu remained motionless, her eyes hidden beneath the green shade. Her two assistants seemed to be petrified.

One of the players suddenly cursed. It was not a pretty sound, and the sullen, indignant murmur that followed it was uglier still. Above it the girl's clear almost raucous voice said:

'All right, boys. The bank admits it's wrong and is paying out.'

'You can't do it, Lulu,' burst out the green-eyed man.

'I'm running this,' said the girl curtly. 'Split the odds. Go on – pay out.'

The man shrugged and began to shove stacks of chips across the oilcloth. He did not flinch as Jed, who had wormed his way quietly around the back, relieved him of his gun. He took the young man's too. 'I'll trust you, Lulu,' he said with a leer on his monkey-face.

He joined his two partners. 'You know where to get your hardware if you want it,' said Oakie. He scooped up his chips and turned away from the table.

Jed and Lon followed his example. The latter turned and looked straight at the girl. She seemed to be watching him, but what her dark eyes held behind the green shade he could not tell.

The three men cashed their chips. 'Would you like to look the town over, Hank?' said Oakie.

'Sure thing,' said 'Hank Blundell'.

'We can show you the town, but there ain't nothin' else we can show you I guess,' said Oakie with a ponderous wealth of meaning in his deep voice. 'Come on.'

They passed the table at which sat Hiram Vanberger and his boys. Lon Burton's eyes raked the four of them and received only looks of arrogant disinterest in return.

THREE

The three men passed into the half-glow of the Virginia City night.

More riders were coming in all the time, carriages too – most of them from the slopes of the mountains where there were mansions of logs and frame and plaster, and even bricks. Stout, florid prosperous-looking men in broad-cloth and women wrapped around with satins, silks, frills and furbelows. Flashing with jewellery and paint and smelling to high heaven.

Oakie pointed out a black and gold closed carriage drawn by four strapping greys.

'There's Cy Carpenter,' he said. 'They say his mine is petering out. But you wouldn't think so to look at Cy. I guess he's got plenty to fall back on anyway. The woman with him is Blanche Delacroix. She useter keep a sporting-house right here in Main – it's Larkin's hash-house now. She had some o' the purtiest gels in the territory, an' she was the belle of the lot. She'd come up the hard way – came from the Golden Gates – and had worked her way up to where she didn't have to mill with the rest of the girls but could play favourites. She had two-three, then Cy came along. He was *it* with

24

Blanche I guess – even before he made his big strike. He built her that big brick house on the slopes in front of his mine – Carpenter's Castle they call it – an' they even got married.'

'Do tell,' said Lon Burton.

'Yeh,' said Oakie. 'I guess Blanche an' Cy are on their way to the Palace Hall. There's a big shindig on. We wasn't invited but we'll look in later if you like, Hank.'

Lon Burton shrugged. 'You're the guide,' he said.

The three men made the rounds of the gambling hells, the saloons and the sporting-houses. Shiner passed them leading a horse and grinned vacuously.

'There he goes,' said Oakie.

The big man was talking all the while. He knew everybody and seemed to know everything that went on. Voluble though he was, he never gave a hint of what his own business might be in Washoe. It seemed to Lon Burton that the big man was biding his time. What was his 'game'?

It was almost midnight when they landed up in Larkin's hash-house. The town was humming like a hive of angry hornets, with a colony of bullfrogs and a batch of yelling coyotes thrown in for good measure. It was Saturday night, and nobody wanted to go to bed – leastways not to sleep anyhow! There was a rumour that a man had been killed in a fight down at the stables and another one was dying with a bullet in the belly after a fight over one of the girls at Madame Kroner's place. The place was swarming with law-deputies with low-slung guns, but it seemed like it was their night off too.

The three men were tipsily merry, and Oakie said:

'What say we do, Hank – go corral us some gels or gatecrash the Palace Hall?'

Lon Burton spat. He said: 'I ain't seen but one gel in this burg who I'd like to give a tumble, an' she looks as cold as a bullfrog's belly. I say the Palace every time.'

'The Palace it is,' grinned Oakie. 'Finish off that cawfee, Jed, 'fore you go to sleep. Shake your pins, man.'

Jed grunted and lurched to his feet. He hiccupped.

'The Palace,' he burbled and followed the other two out.

Lon had a hard task to keep up with Oakie's pace. The big fellow jerked himself forward with long flat-footed strides, his head sunk into his huge shoulders. He looked like he was spoiling for a fight. The Palace was at the bottom of Main Street. Lon remembered passing it on his way in. It had been quiet then, whereas now in direct contrast, the elaborate false-front, painted in a variety of brilliant colours, was garish in the light of a dozen or more flickering naphtha flares. The windows below blazed with light, and one wing of the huge double doors was wide open, sending a stream of light across the wheel-rutted street.

Lon caught up with Oakie, passed him and made a bee-line for the doors. He was teetering a little on his high heels. The big man grabbed his arms.

'That ain't the way to get in,' he said. 'I know a better way than that around the side.'

Lon turned and regarded him, his eyes owlish in the light. He hiccupped – then tapped his lips with gravity and said: 'Pardon.'

Jed, charging along in the rear, cursed as he cannoned into Oakie.

'Quit shovin',' said the big fellow. 'Come on – follow me.'

He changed direction and plunged on. Jed followed him. Then he turned swiftly, almost throwing himself off balance. 'Hey, c'mon, Hank,' he bawled.

Hank stood still, etched leanly against the light, his feet spread, a dogged look on his face.

'Hey, Oakie,' yelled Jed. 'Hank ain't comin'.'

Oakie turned. Then he retraced his steps ponderously. 'Are yuh throwing my invitation back in my face, young fellah?' he asked with gravity.

Lon shook his head, pouted like a child. 'Fine way to welcome a man,' he said. 'Asking him to come in the back way. When I go to a dance I allus enter by the front door. I've hoofed it in finer places than this barn, believe me.' He made a circular gesture with his thumb, taking in the whole façade of the Palace, dismissing it as so much garbage. Then he shrugged. 'Still I guess this'll do for now.' He drew back his shoulders and with a deliberately mincing walk, which was still a mite unsteady, marched forward.

The other two exchanged glances. Then Oakie shrugged and followed in the young man's wake. His little shifty eyes trying to look in every direction at once, Jed followed him.

The Palace had a wide lobby with a high desk and chairs and smaller double-doors which led into the hall proper. Folk were sitting about on the chairs, and at the desk was an oldster with a white goatee beard and a hard-faced man in grey broadcloth.

Lon marched toward the second doors. The old-timer called out: 'Where's yuh invite, young fellah?'

27

Lon took no notice of him and marched on. The hard-faced man in broadcloth left the desk and stood in his path.

'Get out of the way, brother,' said Lon.

The man stood his ground then, as Lon got nearer, his hand reached inside the breast of his jacket.

The young man did not pause in his stride but came forward on the balls of his feet. His fist swung up from his side and hit the hard-faced man squarely on the chin. The man rocked on his heels. Lon reached out with his other hand and grabbed a beautiful grey lapel. He held the dazed man while he reached inside his coat and brought out the wicked-looking .32 he carried. He tucked it into his belt. The man pawed at him, swinging wildly. Lon rode the blow and let him have another one on the button. This time he let him go down, and he hit the floor with a crash. The old-timer, coming out of his trance, lugged something shiny from beneath his desk.

'Hold it, pop,' growled Oakie.

The oldster placed the sawn-off gently in front of him.

'What's this,' he said. 'A stick-up?'

'We just want to go into the dance, old-timer,' said Lon mildly.

He stepped over the unconscious form of the hard-faced man in broadcloth and went through the doors from whence came the music and sound of laughter, clapping, and milling feet.

His gun dangling in his hand, Oakie looked around him. Jed's hand was on the butt of his gun, there was a fearsome scowl on his monkey-face. Nobody said

28

anything or did anything. Oakie looked at Jed and shrugged.

He crossed to the desk, picked up the oldster's shot-gun, emptied it and put the shells in his pocket.

'Sorry we got to do this, pop,' he said. 'We came in peace. I must apologise for the hastiness of my young friend. He's only just arrived in town. I guess he ain't used to havin' to have invites to dances.' He took a bill from his pocket and dropped it on the desk. 'Mebbe that'll cover it.'

The old man opened a drawer, swept the crumpled bill into it. 'I'll see what I can do, Mr Jones.' Then his eyes alighted on the recumbent form on the floor, and he shook his head dolefully. 'Though what Epworth'll do when he wakes up I dunno.'

'Gimme the word if he fetches the law, pop.'

'I'll do that, Mr Jones.'

Oakie turned to Jed. 'We better go see what our little hell-raiser's doin' now, uh?'

The two men passed into the hall. They were relieved to find that everything, as yet, seemed to be under control. The dancers, a shifting blaze of colour, were whirling around to a waltz.

Oakie and Jed scanned the floor anxiously. Finally they spotted their pard, Hank, on the edge of the crowd. He was standing with an inane look on his face watching the dancers and tapping his foot to the music. They wormed their way round and joined him.

'Mr Blundell,' said Oakie owlishly. 'This yere is my friend Jed Crample. Mr Crample – Mr Blundell.'

'Charmed,' said Lon and bowed over Mr Crample's horny hand. Mr Crample sniggered and said nothing.

He looked more like an ape than ever.

At this juncture a young gentleman in faultless evening dress accosted the three men. 'I'm afraid you gentlemen will have to stash your guns,' he said in very polite cowboy talk. 'Jest get a ticket for them at the office over there.' He looked down at Lon's feet. 'Your spurs too, if you don't mind, suh. Mighty dangerous in a crowd.'

Lon bent and unbuckled his spurs. He made a deep bow then placed them gently in the young man's hand.

'My spurs you may have,' he said. 'Though it grieves me deeply to part with them.' Then he leaned forward and crooked his finger. The young man raised his eyebrows and did a smart bend himself. In a stage whisper Lon said:

'I'm afraid that if I give you my guns I'd fall over. You wouldn't want me to make a mess on your nice polished floor would you?'

'I'm afraid that goes for the three of us,' said Oakie entering into the spirit of the thing. 'I dunno how we'd manage to balance without our guns.' He patted his breast. 'Mine's tucked away in bed, an' I'd sure hate to disturb him.'

The young man looked from one to the other of them: at Lon's lean dark face and over-bright eyes, at Oakie's florid beefiness, at Jed's ferocious monkey features. Then he shrugged and turned away.

Oakie nudged Lon. 'Look, there's Blanche Delacroix an' Cy Carpenter, the folks who passed us in the coach. Over there.'

Lon followed the direction of his gaze, and he saw a large, handsome woman with raven-black hair, a glittering comb atop it that must have cost a fortune – if it was real. One plump white hand, the arm above festooned with glistening bracelets, rested on the arm of the tall dark man beside her. He had flapping jowls and sported a black walrus moustache.

Lon sized them up then his eyes passed on to the girl who stood with them and to whom both of them were talking. She was almost as tall as Blanche Delacroix but slimmer. Her hair was sweeping and honey gold beside the other's elaborate black curls. There was no ornament in it except what might have been a tiny red rose above one ear. There were no bangles or clasps on her slim white arms, nothing at her throat where the old-gold satin of the dress met the creamy flesh.

Despite this lack of ostentation however it seemed to Lon Burton's drink-sodden imagination that there was something bold and gamin-like about the set of the girl's perfectly modelled face, about the light in the wide blue eyes. Anyway, what was she doing with a woman like Blanche Delacroix, who had been a 'chippie' on the Barbary Coast, had kept a sporting-house in Virginia City, hell-hole of the West, and lived with Cy Carpenter, aye and many more, before she finally married the dark walrus-looking cuss?

'Who's the filly?' said Lon Burton.

Oakie's brow wrinkled. 'Dunno,' he said. 'Cain't say I've ever seen her before. Certainly is a fetchin' lookin' piece.'

'Yeh,' said Lon. 'I crave me a dance with that young lady.'

'Watch your step, Hank,' said Oakie, but it was

doubtful whether the young man heard him: he was already wending his way through the crowd in the general direction of Cy Carpenter and his little party. Oakie gave another of his ponderous shrugs and with the faithful Jed still at his heels made his way by a more complicated route.

He watched young 'Hank Blundell' all the while, saw him approach the trio, give a little bob in the direction of black Blanche and then face the girl. He saw her eyebrows raise; he saw the black look Cy Carpenter gave the brash young cowboy. Then Hank had moved towards the girl, and, still wide-eyed, she was swept into the crowd.

Carpenter's face went a shade darker, and he started after them. His wife, Blanche, clutched his arm, and he halted and looked down at her. Big woman though she was, he topped her by a good many inches. She looked up at him with her proud dark gaze. She was still a beautiful woman. She suddenly burst out laughing; even from where he stood Oakie heard the richness of it, and the flash of her white even teeth sent a sudden stab to his breast.

He turned away quickly to look for Hank and his partner in the crowd. Finally he spotted them right in the centre of the milling bunch. The band was playing one of those fancy new jigs, and to Oakie the dancers looked like a herd of critturs milling in a corral. He could not get a good look at the young couple, but it seemed like they were talking. The girl was still wide-eyed – though maybe that was her natural state.

Had Oakie but known it she had not yet gotten over her surprise. She had not had chance to answer 'yes' or 'no' to the dark young man's request when she was grabbed, not ineptly, by strong arms and whisked into the crowd.

When she finally got her breath back she said frigidly: 'I don't think we've been introduced have we?'

'That's easily taken care of,' said the young man with a grin. 'I'm Hank Blundell.'

It seemed to her that he had been about to call himself something else, something beginning with L, but had suddenly changed his mind.

'What is your name, fair maid?' he said, and she realized he was more than a little drunk. She could smell it on him, and his talk was a little thick; his gait was unsteady too, he was leaning on her more than was necessary. He was too close.

She said: 'My name is no concern of yours. I'd be obliged, sir, if you would take me from the floor, more carefully and with less speed than you brought me on. Might I point out that you did not have my permission to do so in the first place.'

The young man gaped and was temporarily nonplussed by such a flowery reprimand. It seemed to sober him up a little, and when he finally spoke he sounded almost sheepish.

'Do you come from back East, miss?'

'That also is no concern of yours, sir,' she said. Her tones were icy now, she arched her body away from him, her head held high, her lips curling. 'Take me from the floor immediately. I do not wish to create a scene.'

The rather cloudy eyes in the dark face above her suddenly blazed. The young man seemed to be

33

suddenly terribly angry – more angry than her words had warranted.

He said between clenched teeth: 'You don't want to create a scene, uh? You want to go back quietly to Mama Delacroix. Who do yuh think you're trying to high-hat, my fine filly, uh?' With a brutal gesture he jerked her closer to him. His face was close to her, and she smelled the liquor-fumes on his breath.

Something had pressed into her side. She pulled furiously away from him again and, looking down, realized he had a gun strapped to his waist. She went cold. Without a doubt he was the only man on the floor with a gun. And he looked quite capable of using it if he was roused. She glanced across towards the man and woman she had just left. Cy Carpenter's face wore a heavy scowl, and Blanche's a worried frown. The expression made her look ten years older.

The young man's arms were taut around the girl. He danced stiffly as if he was holding himself in. The savage light had gone from his eyes, but his face was blank, unfriendly.

She said: 'Maybe I was a little too hasty. We will finish this dance. But next time you ask me I hope you will wait for my reply.'

He bowed slightly. 'You're being very generous, miss,' he said.

There was a sneer in his voice, almost a note of hatred.

She wondered what had changed him so suddenly from the jocular, half-drunken young cowboy to the unpleasant man he now was. Surely her quite understandable indignation was not the cause of it. He was

a very unreasonable young man and had spoken of her
two companions in a markedly slighting manner. Had
he, for some reason or other, a grudge against them?

FOUR

Oakie Jones turned to Jed Crample and said: 'Wal, they seem to be settlin' down to it.'

'I've got an idea they ain't gonna be settled-down long,' said Jed.

They were the first words he had spoken for quite a while, but they were fraught with meaning. Oakie followed the direction of his monkey-faced pard's baleful stare.

The tall young man in faultless evening dress was crossing towards Cy Carpenter. Behind him were three other big young men.

'I had an idea he wouldn't forget us,' said Oakie.

'Cy Carpenter's makin' sure the big galoot don't forget Hank anyway,' said Jed.

The dance was coming to an end as the four young men, after a hurried consultation with the big walrus-moustached Carpenter, spread out on the edge of the floor before him and his wife.

The dance finished, the dancers swirled, broke, began to drift away in their separate pieces, each lady on the arm of her swain. Each lady except one.

The blonde lady in the shimmering dress of old-gold

broke away suddenly from her partner. Hastening to follow her, Lon found himself confronted by the young man in faultless evening-dress, who did not look as polite now as he had at their first meeting.

Neither did he act polite: he flung a punch from somewhere down by his knees. It was a scramble, but Lon managed to block it. He flung a retaliatory blow, but this was blocked in its turn, and Lon realized he was up against no mean mauler. He sagged at the knees, one foot spread out before the other; the faultless young man's next haymaker whistled harmlessly by. Lon drove bunched knuckles hard into an unprotected middle. His satisfied grunt was out-classed by his opponent's horrid belching gulp. It was the faultless young man's turn to sag; he sagged right into a straight left which cannoned him into one of his pardners who was advancing to join the fray.

Lon realized what he was up against. He went for his gun. Too late he spotted the burly form on his flank. He was half-turning, his gun half out of its holster when a rock-hard fist exploded on his ear. The lights of the hall made a kaleidoscope around him, and he hit the floor with a crash which made his bones rattle.

The lights became static again; he squirmed away from a swinging boot and rose on all fours, half running, like a coyote with his tail between his legs. He felt sick and dizzy. He put that down to the liquor he had drunk rather than the blow he had received. He had taken worse than that without effect.

He scrambled to his feet and turned. There was a big fellow almost on top of him: a fist which felt like a charge of buckshot slammed him on the shoulder. His heels screeched on the polished floor, he crashed into an onlooker. A woman screamed.

Thankful for the buffer, he used it, charging at his opponent, head down. The manoeuvre was unexpected. The other man received the charge full in the chest. He said 'Ouf' as he was bowled over. Unable to stop himself. Lon charged on and landed head-first in the middle of the crowd. From there he was propelled back onto the floor.

'Go it, younker,' yelled somebody. Evidently not all the guests were 'stuffed shirts'.

He glanced around him swiftly. The man he had charged was lying on his back, his mouth opening and closing like a fish out of water. The faultless young man was being helped to his feet by another, equally fault-lessly attired. The only immediate peril was the stocky young man, not quite so faultless but very competent-looking, who was advancing flat-footed, his fists held in front of him in the correct fighting stance.

Lon flung a glance around him. He could not see Oakie and Jed anywhere. He heard a woman's voice say 'stop them' and saw that it belonged to his golden-haired beauty. To hell with her, he thought, as he charged.

Through slit eyes he saw his opponent move quickly to meet him. He slapped his feet down hard and came to a dead stop. He saw the look of surprise blossom on the other's face, then his fist smashed through the fancy guard and full onto the other's jaw. The face dissolved in blood – then vanished.

Lon gave a whoop and faced about to receive the onslaught of the two faultless young men. They halted

38

warily, then began to circle. Their eyes flickered, and Lon whirled again. He was tackled by another man who flung himself from the crowd.

He winced as his knuckles cracked on a hard head, then he felt himself falling. Hands grabbed him roughly, preventing him. He got in another satisfying blow on flesh which gave beneath his knuckles. Then his arms were pinioned.

He tried to reach his gun but discovered that his holster was empty. He was lifted, spreadeagled, and carried with the floor bobbing a few inches below his face.

It was in the lobby that he broke free once more as one of the men slackened the grip on his legs, allowing him to lash out. He was rewarded by hearing the man yelp with pain, then he had one foot on the floor and levered himself forward with it. He was swinging between two men; they let him go and he went sprawling, his knuckles scraping the floor. He rolled over, jumping cat-like to his feet. Behind the desk he saw the oldtimer with the goatee. The man Lon had kicked was sitting on the floor, his face white. The other two were standing still. Len turned instinctively. The hard-faced man, the one he had slugged in this very lobby not so long back, was advancing on him with uplifted gun.

Lon backed away. He was unarmed, and he knew the hard-faced man did not mean to shoot. His intentions were plain. As his shoulder hit the wall Lon felt something akin to panic. To be pistol-whipped was the most degrading punishment any Westerner could receive. Though many had not lived to savour the fullness of its

39

disgrace. And there was something in the hard-faced man's little black eyes which spelled 'murder'. Incongruously Lon suddenly wondered where the man had gotten that huge Frontier model Colt, so different to the .38 he had sported earlier. That was back somewhere in the hall.

Then the big man moved in; the gun flashed in the light; Lon ducked and heard the barrel crash on the wall behind him. He tried to butt the man, but his other arm was there, guarding himself. Lon flung two blows at the broadcloth-covered middle. It was hard, and though one of the blows sank home it did not seem to have the required effect.

Lon grappled with the man. He had a confused glimpse of the gaping oldtimer, who seemed to be trying to say something, and the three men who had brought him out: they were motionless, hazy-like figures in a dream. Then the barrel of the gun bit into his shoulder. He stifled a cry and, in a spasm of blinding rage, brought up his knee.

He heard the big man grunt with pain. He shoved him away and dived for the outer doors. One of the three men came alive and came at him with a flying tackle. Lon kicked out, felt the toe of his boot jar home. But the man's hurtling body crashed into him, sending him flying back once more against the wall.

The big man charged, swinging the gun. Lon bobbed and weaved, trying to dodge that swinging arm and get under it at the same time. The heavy gun descended on his right bicep muscle. Hot pain flared through his arm, then it became dead and useless. Lon struck savagely, desperately, with the other one. Then the

40

gun-barrel caught him a glancing blow across the temple.

As he reeled away a film of blood blanketed his eyes. His enemy assumed a giant's proportions, and the swinging arm was a lever beating him down – down.

He felt pain again. In his body, in his face, in his head. He thought he heard a voice shouting: 'Stop it! Stop it!' It sounded like a woman's voice.

Then blackness shut out every sight and every sound. Sick reeling blackness. Then nothingness. Nothing at all.

When he came-to the cool night air was blowing on his face. He was lying in the street, and Oakie and Jed were bending over him.

'Where've you two jaspers been?' he said.

'Discretion is the better part of valour,' quoted Oakie succinctly.

Jed, as usual when weighty matters were in hand, said nothing.

Lon said: 'Fine pardners you turned out to be.' His head felt as big as two and his body like it had been mounted on a bucking bronc for a couple of hours. He was inclined to be querulous.

'I might've bin killed,' he said.

'You nearly were,' said Oakie. 'An', believe me, Jed an' I were all set to step in an' even things up with our irons when the girl called that big pistol-swinging skunk off'n yuh.'

'What girl?'

'The girl you danced with.'

'Her!' said Lon, then, after a mite of reflection: 'I

RED SILVER!

guess she didn't want any blood on her hands.'

'Whether or not she certainly laced that big fellah with her tongue. Boy, it was real purty.'

'Pity you weren't able to hear it,' said Jed.

'While nobody was looking we carted you out here,' said Oakie.

'That was mighty nice of you,' was the cynical rejoinder. Lon began to get up and groaned.

The two men helped him to his feet. 'Sorry we had to kind of run out on yuh,' said Oakie. 'It don't do for me to get mixed up in such shindigs.'

'Oh, it don't, uh? Might I ask why?'

'I'll explain that later. Anyway, we had our eye on yuh in case things got too hot.'

Lon, limping along between them, his hands resting on a shoulder each side, said:

'Wal, you certainly saved me from bein' completely frazzled.'

'The gel stepped in jest 'fore we did—'

'To hell with the girl!'

Oakie changed the subject. 'C'mon up to my place an' we'll fix you up.'

The progress was slow up the hill. Lon felt like he wanted to lie down and crawl along on his belly. He was weak; filled with hatred for that golden-haired girl and that black walrus *hombre* Cy Carpenter and the hard-faced man who had wielded the cruel Colt. Strangely enough he came last on the list, and the other attackers not at all. He put all the blame on the girl and that smarmy pimp, Carpenter. It did not occur to him to attach any blame to himself.

Nobody took much notice of them as they progressed

42

up the hill. A few people greeted Oakie and Jed.

They reached the big houses, the 'Nob Hill' of Virginia City, but Oakie did not pause there: he carried on, and their climb became steeper. Lon's toes dragged on the ground; the other two were half-carrying him; he realized he had taken a real grandaddy of a beating. What a welcome to Washoe!

'F'r Pete's sake, how much further?' he groaned. 'Where do you live – up on the peak?'

'Just another short piece, Hank,' Oakie told him. As he spoke they reached what seemed to be the end of the street. The mountains loomed over them.

'He lives in a cave,' groaned 'Hank'.

'That pile's further away than it looks.' Oakie veered suddenly to the left and continued to climb. They reached a dark jumble of huts overlooking the clustered lights of the town. It was to one of the larger of these huts that Oakie led Lon and opened the door with a key he produced on the end of a chain at his vest. Jed slipped inside first. 'Take it easy, Hank.' said Oakie.

Flame blossomed as Jed lit the lamp. The interior of the place was suddenly illuminated. Stabs of pain shot through Lon's eyeballs, and for a moment everything swam around him. Then his vision cleared. He saw the planed log walls, the heavy old furniture which seemed top heavy and bulging, too big for the place, the stone fireplace, the deal table with the remains of a meal, incongruous amid the rest of the stuff, the rag mats on the dirty board floor.

Oakie led him over to a huge horse-hair couch from which the stuffing was dribbling in a dozen places.

43

'Park here,' he said.

Lon sagged down. Tall though he was, as he perched on the couch his feet only just reached the floor. He leaned his head on the rough back and tried to collect his senses. He was wary; he wished his head did not spin so much; he remembered that he had not known these two men a few hours ago, and still he knew nothing about them. The beating, although it had scattered his faculties, had sobered him up. He remembered why he had come to Virginia City in the first place and was savage because he had let himself become side-tracked. He was a drunken skunk. He began to think about the girl. He wondered what her name was. She had thought him a drunken skunk too. Who did she think she was anyway? To hell with her!

Jed came across to him and gave him a tin mug full of raw whisky. He tossed it back in one gulp. It went inside him like a stream of liquid fire, blossoming like rain in his stomach almost as if someone had stabbed him there. Then the pain cleared and he felt better, whole again, his smarting wounds only sharpening his senses.

'Have you got a mirror?' he said.

Jed went away, then returned with a cracked shaving mirror. Lon turned his face to the light and looked at himself. One of his ears was swollen and blood-stained; there was a jagged line of red across his temple and a bruise on his cheekbone. He did not look pretty but was perfectly recognizable. His shoulder and upper arm were stiff but there was nothing broken.

Oakie appeared through a door at the back. He

44

carried a bowl of steaming water and a few strips of cloth.

'I figured you wouldn't want a doc messing with yuh,' he said. 'Anyway I had a bit of practise in nursin' durin' the war.'

'I don't need no nursing,' said Lon.

'You be ruled by me, Hank,' said Oakie. 'The chemicals from the mines an' the dust from the stamping-mills that's floating about in the air in this burg ain't good for no wounds. You'd better have a plaster on that ear an' that head.'

He placed the bowl of water on the corner of the table, tore a piece from the cloth and dipped it, brought it out dripping and steaming, then wrung it out almost dry.

'Hold your haid still.'

FIVE

Oakie had changed. He was sober now, more like the stern-looking man who had shooed Shiner away on the steps of The Venus Bar. As he ministered to Lon Burton's hurts the lean young man's brain was racing. Why was this man taking so much trouble with a stranger? His beefy face was grim now: he did not look like a Good Samaritan – or the sort to warble 'Welcome to Washoe' to any Tom, Dick or Harry who happened along. He looked like he could be a mighty ugly customer at a pinch. That went for his ape-like pard too!

As Oakie bent over Lon his broadcloth suit bulged where the shoulder-holster sagged. Lon winced as the warm wet cloth passed over his battered ear. He said:

'Who was the buzzard who tried to pistol-whip me?'

'Joe Epworth. He's a supervisor at Cy Carpenter's mine. In the swim. He allus stands guard – to keep out the riff-raff – when they have one o' them shindigs.'

' "Riff-raff",' snorted Lon. 'What do they think *they* are?'

'Money's power, son,' said Oakie. 'I guess they think they're tops. An' right now I guess they are.' He leaned a little closer. There was something in his eyes that

46

gave the young man a tickle down his spine.

'You don't like them folks do you, Hank?'

'What folks?'

'Carpenter an' his woman an' the rest of 'em.'

'I don't know 'em, but, everything considered, I guess I don't exactly love 'em.'

'Maybe you'll have a chance to get back at 'em – Joe Epworth an' all.'

'How come.'

'Listen,' said Oakie. He perched himself on the edge of the table. He looked around him then made a sweeping gesture with his arm.

'I sold up a thrivin' little hoss-ranch to come to this hell-forsaken hole. The silver-bug had bitten me – I thought I could be a millionaire in a week. Jed was the only one of the boys who'd come with me. I guess the others were right – they're better off risking their necks on killer-stallions than waiting to get a bullet or a knife in the back in Virginia City.'

He made that sweeping movement again. 'I bought this stuff at a sale at one o' the big houses. Got it for next to nothin'. The owner had a mine which stopped running suddenly – no more bonanza. He found himself in debt up to his ears. He shot himself.' Oakie shrugged. 'Oh yes, I've got what I came for. I've got a little mine – behind us there. My trouble is that I can't get men to work it. Right now, besides me an' Jed, I've got three men workin' for me. Oh, I pay 'em all right – I pay 'em better than any other owner in Washoe. Only things happen to 'em when they work for me—'

'How come?'

Oakie leaned forward and splayed out his fingers.

47

'The big boom's over. Many of the smaller bonanzas have petered out. People are grabbin' all they can and lightin' out. Others with less sense are digging some-place else. An' all the time folks are pourin' into Washoe thinkin' they can pick silver up in the streets. There are three big mines right on top of the town.' He ticked them off on his fingers: 'Carpenter's, Pop Quail's an' Hiram Vanberger's. There's rumours that Vanberger's bonanza is petering out. Whether they're true or not I haven't been able to find out. One thing I do know however is that all three of these owners pay their men starvation wages and make them work like slaves under the worst possible conditions. I move in, I pay the men reasonable wages, I listen to their complaints, I try to make my place a fit place to work in.' Oakie paused.

He went on: 'Why, when I first got here, when I first found my bonanza, I could have had as many men as I wanted. They were clamouring to work for me. Then things began to happen to my men; they got beat up, they got shot at. A few of 'em got killed. Then I knew the rest of the owners didn't like the way I did things. They wanted to run me out. I got shot at, I had a boul-der roll down the mountainside and nearly smash me, I had a couple of hired gunmen throw down on me on Main Street. They'd've got me too if Jed hadn't moved in behind 'em. That's why I didn't mix in that shindig at the Palace – an' maybe give somebody a chance to slide a knife between my ribs or trip me an' kick my head in. I guess almost everybody there was an enemy o' mine one way or another – murderers too, for all their fancy clothes—'

'Why tell me all this?'

48

Oakie did not answer that question right off. Instead he asked one himself.

'Why did you come to Virginia City, Hank?'

'To look for a job.'

'What kind of a job? You come from Texas way, don't yuh? Beef – roughridin' – ain't nothin' like that here, Hank. What kind of a job?'

'Maybe I thought I'd find me a silver mine same as you.'

Oakie looked him up and down. The long lank black hair, the dark sloe eyes, the high cheekbones, slightly hooked nose and thin tight lips. The lean deep-chested body, the thick gunbelt.

'You don't look to me like the sort of gink to work on a mine. Not the sort of gink to get any pleasure sweatin' for that kind of money. It's a long ways from Texas – though I'm figuring that ain't the only place you've been.'

'You could be right.'

Oakie leaned forward. He said: 'Me an' Jed saw you ride into town. We saw you standin' on the boardwalk in front o' The Venus an' look the town over. We saw the way you acted when that hoss fell in a pothole an' its rider kicked it. I said to myself there's a man who's bin around guns and hosses ever since he was knee-high to a grasshopper – an' knows how to handle 'em. Then Shiner happened along, an' I figured you weren't the sort he could meddle with so I stopped him. Then when I heard you talk I figured you for a Texan.'

'You're quite a detective, Oakie.'

'Am I? – Why not work for me, Hank?'

'A minute ago you said I wouldn't fit in at a mine,

49

that I wouldn't sweat for that kind o' money. I guess you're right, though I must admit I took a liking for this town right away, an' I sure ain't aimin' to mosey on again yet awhile. Now you're askin' me to work for you – where would I fit into your mine?'

'You wouldn't have to go anywhere near the mine.' Oakie paused. His brow crinkled. 'I've taken a liking to you, Hank.' He paused again, turned to Jed. 'Gimme that gun.'

From somewhere in the shadows behind him Jed produced a Colt .45 and handed it over. With a start of surprise Lon realized it was his own. Oakie gave it to him.

'We managed to pick it up,' he said. He shut his mouth tightly then, and his little eyes were fixed on the cowboy.

Lon said. 'I get it now: you want me to tote a gun for you.'

'Shall we say I want you to do a little investigating for me. An' I'll pay you a damsight more than any poor sweatin' devil workin' underground.'

'I've done lots o' things, but I don't think I've ever sold my gun before.'

'I guess folks've bought it though maybe you didn't know it at the time. I've seen you in action . . . . You fought in the war?'

'Yep.'

Oakie's voice was very quiet when he spoke again. 'This time you can be sure you're fighting on the winning side. I mean to win!'

Lon weighted his gun in his hand. 'What would I do first?'

50

Again Oakie did not answer the question right off. He said: 'I think if I get one good man like you to stick by me others will automatically follow.'

'You don't know anythin' about me.'

'I'm takin' a chance on you. I know Virginia City – you don't.' Oakie's meaning was very plain.

'I mightn't last long enough for you to get reinforcements,' said Lon drily.

'You'll last.'

Lon repeated his question. 'What would I do first?'

Before replying Oakie turned and looked at Jed. The monkey-faced man was in the shadows by the door. He did not move.

Oakie perched on the table, swung his leg and surveyed the dusty toe of his boot reflectively. He said:

'Hiram Vanberger is the leader of those who are against me. He's the driving force. Cy Carpenter is busy havin' himself a good time – he has to be pushed into things. Pop Quail is getting old. Them two fight me as a matter of course, but Vanberger hates me. He started from the bottom like me. He worked his way up on the backs of others – scores of men have died in his mine. It's notorious for bad conditions – he has a mob of hired gunmen to keep the workers docile. Maybe, like they say, he's finishing. Maybe he'd like to take over this place. Either way, now is the time to get him.'

'Get him?'

'His gunmen tried to get me. Jed fixed 'em. But there's plenty more where they came from, an' I guess it's near time they had another go. You saw those three who were with Vanberger tonight?'

'Yeh.'

51

'They're always with him an' they have the reputation of being reg'lar hellions. Vanberger's handy with a gun himself – though you maybe wouldn't think so – which makes four of 'em against Jed an' me. In the ordinary way o' things we can take care of ourselves, but four professionals is too many to tackle. Now if there was three of us instead o' two – an' we got the inside edge.' Oakie stopped talking and spread his hands eloquently.

Lon Burton spun the chamber of his gun. He took two shells from his belt and shoved them into empty sockets. He rose as he holstered the gun, he flexed his shoulder and swung his arm experimentally.

'Maybe I oughta fix that,' said Oakie softly.

'No, it'll be all right. I feel fine.' Lon turned and looked full at the big man. 'I'll think over your proposition, Oakie,' he said. 'I'll let you know.'

The big man shrugged. 'All right, boy. Take your time.'

The young man crossed to the door. Jed stood in his path. There was a ferocious scowl on his monkey-face.

Lon threw his weight on to the balls of his feet. His spine pricked. His rear was unprotected. Nobody would hear a shot up here. He looked at Jed's eyes, saw them shift, gaze over his shoulder. Jed stepped aside. Lon said: 'Thanks f'r everythin', boys,' and passed out into the night.

He walked down the hill into Main Street, a lean cowboy mincing on high-heeled boots, long arms brushing his sides, hat tipped over his eyes to hide bandages. He sniffed the air, dust and fume laden, he looked back

at the mountain brooding over everything like an evil
spirit. What was it about this town that got him? It was
filthy, it was cheap, it was bad. It called to something
within him with a call that could not be denied.

Then why hadn't he taken Oakie Jones' offer?

He scanned the big houses as he passed them. It was
Sunday morning now, and the humming was dying
down. Belated carriages toiled up the hill and halted
outside ornate verandahs or turned into dusty drives.

A black and gold closed carriage drawn by four
magnificent greys whirled past him. A face looked out
at him from the window, a pale perfectly modelled face
framed in golden hair. Then it was gone, leaving him
with a strange sense of bewilderment and another feeling he could not define.

He shrugged, tripped delicately over a rut like a
miniature canyon and continued on his way. As he
moved into the bawdy centre of that corner of Nevada
known as Washoe, where folks were still whooping it
up, teamsters playing 'craps' on the sidewalk and
women openly hawking their wares, his steps became
lighter, and he looked around him warily.

He entered The Venus Bar.

The place was not quite so full as earlier that night.
Men who conscientiously objected to going to bed on a
Saturday night had compromised by sleeping under
tables and in shady corners. Lulu Sanclaire was still
running her faro layout, but she had two new assistants. Hiram Vanberger and his retinue still held court
at the centre table.

As before, hard eyes appraised Lon as he passed the
party. If he expected one of their owners to speak he

was disappointed. The band played sleepily.

He shoved his belly against the bar and ordered a straight rye. The barman looked at his bandaged forehead curiously as he served the order.

'Gimme the bottle,' said Lon curtly.

He took three stiff slugs right off. They filled his body with fire and shot him up to the top of the world. He forgot all about the beating he had received.

He crossed to Lulu's layout and got himself a place at the table. The girl looked up.

'Hallo, cowboy,' she said in that clear harsh voice of hers. 'Have you come to catch the bank again?' Lon's eyes rested on her boldly then, as she dropped her head, shielding her expression with the green eyeshade, he said:

'I like the look of your assistants a bit better this time, ma'am. I beg your pardon for any previous inconvenience I may have caused you.'

'Place your bets, cowboy,' said Lulu. It seemed strange to him that she had not spoken to him directly before. Now it seemed almost like they were old friends. Or was that just soft-soap on her part? She certainly owed him something for breaking up the game; costing the bank a packet too.

He looked from one to the other of the two assistants. The case-keeper sported a thin moustache, he was coffee-coloured, probably a Creole. He bowed ironically, no shade of expression in his heavy lidded eyes. The look-out was a palpable gambler. Lon had run into his kind all over the West. He was tall and lean and faultlessly dressed in black. His face looked like a white waxen mask. He bowed too, like an automaton.

Lon had the feeling that if he tried to bust up this game he would have a whole heap of action stacked up against him. Here was a cold-blooded gambling killer if ever there was one. And the Creole didn't look no baby-washer either.

Interest began to centre on the layout once more. Lon had an idea, by the covert glances that were thrown at him, that his presence had something to do with that. There were plenty there who had seen his play earlier that night.

Through a conveniently placed mirror, one of the many which ranged the walls, he watched the Vanberger table. The little mine owner had his back to him, but two of his men were turning and looking this way. One in particular Lon made note of – he had a face like a sick vicious horse, and a livid blue scar ran the whole length of it from temple to jaw.

Concentrating on the game once more, Lon realized he had won. He raked in his chips and bowed slightly at Lulu. She gave no sign.

He placed his bets again. He watched the game keenly, but out of the corner of his eye saw the Vanberger retinue shuffling around as if preparing to take their leave. This time he lost.

Lulu called: 'That's all for tonight, gentlemen. Thank you for your patronage.'

He moved away from the table, back to the bar. He was sipping a drink as he watched the girl, supple, swift-moving in her black dress, mount the side stairs. He saw the three gunmen standing in a group around the centre table: their little boss seemed in no hurry to rise. Lon figured that if he had been drinking steadily all night long he must have a skinful. And not a lot of skin to hold it in either. He was watching the girl going up the stairs, but she vanished, and still he did not rise.

She was not long away and soon reappeared wearing her red cloak. She came down the stairs and across the floor. The crowd parted to let her through. Hiram Vanberger rose and bowed as she passed his table. She did not even glance at him.

Lon Burton grinned, left the bar and followed in the wake of the girl. As he passed the centre table he looked straight at the mine owner. Vanberger's face was expressionless. No flicker of feeling or recognition showed in his little black-button eyes.

As Lon got outside a carriage drew up, a stocky simple-looking man got down and helped Lulu to the seat beside him.

Lon went nearer. 'Miss Sanclaire,' he said.

She looked down at him. For all the expression her eyes held she might have still been wearing the eyeshade. 'Yes?' she said.

'I hope you'll accept my apology for the ruckus I caused earlier tonight.'

'No apology is needed,' she said frigidly. 'Monty was careless. Drive on, Bull.'

Lon Burton was almost thrown to the ground as the carriage started away suddenly. A cloud of dust drifted back into his face.

He cursed fluently. Did every cheap female in Virginia City act like she was royalty?

SIX

He heard the door swing open behind him and, glancing over his shoulder, saw that Vanberger and his three gunmen were coming out. A youth brought a string of four horses along to the front of the place.

'Hurry it up, darn you,' said one of the men.

Lon moved nonchalantly along the boardwalk and turned into the alley which led to the stables. Then he began to move swiftly, light footed in the darkness. He reflected that this was a crazy place for the stables, as black as the pit of hell, a convenient place to sap a man with a pocketful of winnings.

He reached the stable-door. It swung open and light flashed out from the swinging lantern. Instinctively his hand dropped to his gun. Then he saw that the figure in the doorway was Shiner, his queer lidless eyes more than ever pointing the aptness of his nickname.

'Hallo, mister,' said Shiner. 'You want your hoss. I'll get him.'

He turned. Lon followed him, paused, waited.

Shiner led the horse out. Lon said: 'You remembered which one it was then?'

'Yeh I remembered. I saw you come out of The Venus

just now. I guessed you'd want him. I saddled him up for you.'

'That's mighty good of you, Shiner.' Lon took the reins, offered the youth a crumpled bill.

Shiner shook his head. His eyes shone horribly. It seemed to the cowboy that there was a sudden hurt in them.

Shiner said: 'Any pard o' Oakie Jones's is a pard o' mine. Goodnight, mister.'

Next moment he faded into the gloom. Lon shrugged and turned to go. He almost ran into the stable-lad who said: 'Is that pesky half-wit here again?'

'He ain't doin' no harm, son,' said Lon and passed on.

When he reached the end of the alley Vanberger and his men were cantering their horses up the hill. Lon followed at a discreet distance.

Their progress became slower as they climbed. Vanberger was swaying a little in the saddle. Finally, towards the top of Washoe's 'Nob Hill,' they turned into a short drive.

Lon rode on right past, looking at the house as he did so. It lay a few hundred yards back from the street and was surrounded by a rickety picket fence. On the patch of ground beyond some attempt had been made to grow shrubs and small trees, but they had wilted in the poisonous air and seemed to be dying. Behind them the house was like something out of a sick dream.

It had two balconies upstairs, apart from the usual verandah below and looked ludicrously top-heavy. Part of it was of brick, part of it of frame, the whole jumbled together and whitewashed over. The stuff was flaking from the bricks, giving a piebald effect. The two tall chimneys were of brick, stuck on haphazardly as if as an afterthought. They looked like little men with top-hats. The drive led up to the front doors, which were wide and double and painted in a colour which Lon could not make out in the darkness but was darker than the rest of the house.

He saw the mine-owner and one of the men dismount there and climb the steps. The doors were opened by what looked like a negro man, and the two men passed through. The other two led the horses around the side of the house and vanished from sight.

Lon Burton continued to ride slowly. This end of the main drag was quiet now. From time to time he glanced over his shoulder. Finally he saw the two horsemen turn out of the drive and ride back down the street. He watched them till they vanished in the gloom then turned his horse and followed in their wake.

He went past the big house, discovered a convenient waste lot and rode slowly across it. It led him to a cluster of boulders, an outcrop from some disused mine, the shaft of which still gaped open. He dismounted from his horse and ground-hitched him.

He looked about him then, tripping awkwardly on his high-heeled boots, moved along parallel with the rocks. The side of the big house loomed up in front of him, he bellied into the picket-fence. He took a little mincing run and vaulted it.

There was little cover in the grounds. His hand was on his gun as he darted from tree to stunted tree. He reached a wall and flattened himself against it. He wormed along to a window and tried to look in. It was heavily curtained. There was no light there. There was no light anywhere.

He went round the back of the house. A light shone in an upper window. He found a door and tried it. It was locked. He selected the window on the right-hand side of it, took off his hat and wrapped it around his fist and broke the glass with this improvised club.

He stood still then and listened. There was no sound, except from faraway down Main where a bunch of drunken men were singing. He put his hand and forearm through the jagged hole and felt around gingerly.

He found a catch and slipped it out of its socket. He pushed the window open. Again he listened for a moment. Then he climbed through the window. He kicked a pail and the clatter awoke the echoes. He moved along the wall, flattened himself there and waited.

He heard shuffling footsteps and light appeared through the crack beneath the door opposite him. The door swung open slowly. The beams of a lantern illuminated the room, and the ebony face and rolling eyes of the man who held it.

'All right, Sam, stay right there,' Lon said. 'I've got a gun on you.'

The man halted, petrified, the lantern swinging gently in his hand. Lon catfooted across to him, skirting a small table on the way. He took the lantern from the negro's trembling hand and put it on the table. 'Turn around,' he said. 'Put your hands up.'

'Don't shoot, suh, don't shoot.' The man turned slowly around, his hands fluttering upwards.

Lon pressed the barrel of the gun in his back and reached his other hand round in front. He unbuckled the negro's belt. The man's trousers fell down with a rush, revealing his long flannel underpants. He tottered.

Lon held him up, pinioned his arms to his sides with the belt, fastening it tightly. He whipped the man's dirty sweat-cloth from around his neck and crammed it into his mouth. He pulled that tightly.

'Turn around again.'

The negro turned. His mouth was forced wide open by the gag. His white teeth gleamed. His eyes were bulging with terror. Lon pushed the gun against his stomach.

'I hate to do this, Sam.' he said. 'Jest answer me a few questions an' you'll be all right. How many folks are there in the house? Nod your head so many times.' The man nodded his head five times. Lon said:

'How many upstairs?'

The negro nodded his head three times. 'Who are the two down here: the boss and the gunman?'

The man nodded his head frenziedly. 'All right. Get down on your knees. Then lie flat on your belly. I shan't be far away. If you try any funny tricks I'll come back an' plug yuh. Understand?'

Again the kinky head nodded, the big eyes rolled with terror in the glistening black face. Then the man rolled on his stomach. He tried to play possum but could not control the tremors of his body.

Lon blew out the lantern. He went through the door and closed it gently behind him. He stood still to get his eyes accustomed once more to the darkness.

He was in a hallway. There was a very faint glow of light at the other end. Sound too – like a murmur of voices.

He catfooted along the passage and reached the corner. Looking around it he discovered the light came from beneath a door. The murmur of voices was plain now but he could not hear what was being said.

A chair scraped, footsteps sounded. He heard words then a gruff voice saying: 'Goodnight, boss.'

He drew back into the shadows as the door opened. A man passed him: he saw the long white face, the livid blaze of the scar. Then the man turned his head, his eyes widening, his hand dropping. Lon struck out with his gun, felt the barrel jar on bone. He caught the man as he sagged, his bootheels scraping. He lowered him gently to the floor. There was blood on the white horse-face.

Light streamed out as the door opened once more. Lon stood in the shadows and waited. Feet scraped, a querulous voice said:

'Hackett.'

Lon went around the corner, his gun levelled. 'Take it easy, Mike,' he said. 'I came in peace. Get back in there.'

The little man who called himself Hiram Vanberger backed into the room. Lon Burton followed, kicking the door to behind him with his heel. He holstered his gun.

The little man slumped into a huge padded armchair in this book-lined library.

'Lon Burton,' he gasped. 'What—? Where's Hackett?'

'On the first count I'm going by the name of Hank Blundell. If you can change your name I guess I can

62

too. On the second count – if Hackett's the man with the scar, he's sleepin'. He made a hasty movement. You know how I hate hasty movements, Mike.'

'Don't call me Mike.' The little man was regaining confidence, getting a mite puffed up again.

'I've always called you Mike. I came here lookin' for Mike Hanlon, an' I find Hiram Vanberger. A real fancy name that. It suits you. I like Mike best though.'

'What is this – blackmail? You came here lookin' for me? How did you know I was here? What are you after?'

Lon Burton perched himself on the arm of another padded chair. 'You're not very friendly, Mike. You useter be a real friendly cuss when we rode for the Double W together. I allus said, even then, that you weren't cut out for a cowhand. You make a much better mine-owner. I met Loopy Cranston – you remember old Loopy don't you, Mike – he's loopier than ever after workin' for you. He told me you'd struck it rich – you were cock of the dung-heap here. He didn't tell me you'd changed your name. Either way, you're such a big man now I figured you'd be able to find a job for an old pard like me.'

'I ain't got no jobs for trouble-shooters like you – I'm runnin' a legitimate business.' Vanberger shut his mouth suddenly like a trap as if he was sorry he had spoken those last words. He leaned forward in his chair. Suddenly he looked a lot younger, almost as young as the man opposite him. After a pause he said:

'I'm glad to see you, Lon, truly I am; it's quite like old times. I am sorry you've had to be disappointed after coming all this way to see me. You must realize my position though – you're a cowhand, you wouldn't fit into a mine. But I'll do what I can to get you a post in some other line – a wrangler maybe. And if you want any money to tide you over for a bit—'

He delved in his coat and brought out a wallet. He peeled greenbacks off a thick wad.

Lon Burton grinned. 'What's that?' he said. 'Conscience money? Still thinkin' about those cows you stole off ol' man Porter before you left him?'

'You're not going to hold that over my head are you? – that's past.'

'No, I'm not going to hold it over your head. But I ain't forgot it as quickly as you. I nearly took the rap for it myself, remember? I had to leave the Pecos in a hell of a hurry. We wuz pards remember? – folks blamed me as much as you—'

'I'm sorry about that, Lon. I've been wanting to make it up to you—'

'Put your conscience money away, Mike. I don't want any of it—'

Vanberger drew himself up. Once more he was the autocratic little man of the saloon. He said:

'Conscience! You're a fine one to talk about conscience. You'd probably be sitting pretty with me now if it wasn't for that damned conscience of yours.'

'Is that why you don't want to hire me, Mike – because of my conscience? I guess Scarface out there an' his two pardners don't have any, uh? Or any other pet plug-uglies you have on your payroll to keep your mine-slaves in check—'

'You've been snooping.'

'No, I ain't been snooping – but I been keeping my

ears open. I've also been offered a job – by somebody who's out to get you. I didn't take it because we were pards once; I came along to listen to the other side of the question. I don't hafta hear it now. I guess I'll ask you once more: can you find me a job – a straight job – where you won't think you ought to pay me conscience-money?'

'I like you, Lon,' said Vanberger softly. 'I allus have liked you. But I can't offer you any kind of job – an' I'm warning you: don't meddle!'

Lon Burton rose. 'If I have to fight you,' he said. 'I'll fight you on even ground. I'll fight you as if I'd never met you before – you, Hiram Vanberger, me, Hank Blundell.' He was at the door then, and his voice softened. 'It would have been much better to have me on your side, Mike.'

Vanberger did not say anything. Lon closed the door behind him, leapt over the recumbent form of Hackett and ran into the kitchen.

'So-long, Sam,' he said to the negro, and he went out the way he came in.

He mounted his horse and set off at a gallop up Main Street. At the end of it he dismounted from his horse and led him to the left up the steep slope until he came to the mine-workings and the cluster of huts. They were all in darkness. He advanced warily.

He was almost upon the hut he sought when a familiar voice barked:

'All right. Take it easy. Stand still. Unbuckle your belt an' let it drop.'

Lon did as he was told. As his heavy gunbelt scaled away from him he felt almost naked.

'That you, Oakie?' he said.

'Yeh.' The voice was uncompromising.

'Have yuh anywhere a tired cowboy can sleep for the night?'

'That's peaceful talk,' said another voice, belonging to Jed Crample.

Bootheels scraped on the shale. The bulk of Oakie Jones loomed up out of the darkness.

'So you've come back, Hank?'

'Yep.'

'Anybody with yuh?'

'Nope.'

A gun glinted in Oakie's hand. He jerked his head. 'Jed's back there,' he said pointedly.

He bent and picked up Lon's gunbelt. 'Come on,' he said.

Lon followed him. He heard feet scraping and knew the apish Jed was not far behind him. He had those prickles down his spine once more.

Oakie led him to a smaller hut. He swung the door open. 'You can sleep in here,' he said.

'Thanks,' said Lon.

The door slammed behind him. He heard a key turn in a heavy lock. He heard footsteps die away, then there was silence. He realized that Oakie had taken his gun and belt.

He began to feel around. There was no window in the hut, and he could not see a thing. He discovered finally, by a painful process of exploration, that he was in a toolshed of some kind.

He found an old mattress and a pile of blankets in a corner. Evidently somebody had slept here before. He lay down and covered himself up and tried to think.

His head was spinning, his body ached all over. All his wounds began to make themselves felt, and he was very tired. Finally he drifted off into a troubled sleep.

SEVEN

When he awoke he was still in semi-darkness. A chill grey light was seeping beneath the door of the hut. He had not slept long he knew. His mind was still in a turmoil.

He wondered if anything had awakened him, and his hand went up beneath his head, where he always kept his gun when he was sleeping. He realized then what had happened to it and where he was.

His mind became alert but his body was sluggish and stiff as he rose. He crossed to the door and listened. There was no sound from outside. He tried the door. It was still locked.

He went back to the mattress and hankered down upon it with his back against the wall. He felt for his cigarettes, found them, selected a rather battered weed. He searched his pockets for matches but found none. He threw the cigarette away from him with a curse.

What was Oakie's game now? Did he know that Lon had paid a visit to Hiram Vanberger? No, that was impossible. Why the sudden change of front? Oakie was evidently not taking any chances. Even so he was a mighty hard guy to understand. What did he mean to do this morning?

What did Lon himself mean to do? Did he want to mosey away from Washoe – to keep on moseying like he had done for the last few years. Or did he want to stay put? There was something about the place – hell-hole though it was – that had hit him where he lived. Maybe that was because he liked hell-holes – they were more exciting than the ordinary kind. Furthermore in this particular one there was a situation that delighted his reckless soul. He rubbed his face ruefully – also he had a few chores to do before he left – whether it was sooner or later.

He figured that he would not be in shape to take care of anything unless he quit worrying himself to a frazzle and got some sleep.

He lay down and curled up, pulling the dust-stinking blankets up under his chin. In a few seconds he was asleep once more and his breathing was steady and untroubled.

He was awakened by the agonizing creaking of the opening door. He sat bolt upright, looking around him for a weapon. Oakie Jones and Jed Crample came into the hut, the morning sunshine streaming in after them. Neither of them carried a gun. The young man rose to his feet, blinking in the light. At that moment he looked like a rather sulky tousle-haired kid.

Oakie grinned. He said: 'What you aiming to do, Hank?'

'Hank' shrugged and spread his hands. Oakie swung something in his hand. Hank saw it now – his belt and gun.

'I guess nobody's stopping yuh from moseying along. But you're welcome to stay,' said Oakie.

'Changed your tune haven't yuh?'

'A man's got to make sure.'

'Have you made sure?'

'No. I'm still taking a risk.'

'Give me the gun.' Lon held out his hand. Slowly Oakie brought his arm around, held it out in front of him, the gunbelt dangling from the end of it. Lon took it and strapped it around his lean middle. He said:

'I ain't leavin' Virginia City yet. But I ain't promisin' nothin' yet either. If I do decide to work for you I ain't goin' around throwing down on people I owe nothin' to. I like to be provoked before I do my shootin'.'

'That's ethical,' said Oakie. 'But if you start to work for me I guess you'll get provoked sooner or later.'

Lon was silent for a minute. Then he said: 'Anyway I've got a private chore to do in that line first.'

Oakie put his head on one side. 'Joe Epworth?'

'Yeh. Nobody pistol-whips me an' gets away with it.'

'He's fast – but I guess you can haze him. A man's got to go his own way sometimes. You'll find Joe in Larkin's hash-house this morning – between eleven an' twelve. He allus eats there.'

'Thanks, Oakie. Let me go my own way.'

'That's what I said, son.' Oakie stepped aside. Jed followed his example. 'Watch yourself, boy,' he said. Lon passed them.

Oakie called: 'Your hoss's in the old stable jest to the right there.'

The young man did not look back or reply in any way. He went into the stable; the two men were cross-

70

ing to the living-quarters when he led his horse down
the mountain slope. He passed three workmen coming
up, and they looked at him suspiciously. One of them
had a fresh white bandage around his head.

At the bottom of the slope Lon mounted and rode
into Main Street. Already the sun was being obscured
by drifting dust and the stink of chemicals was in the
air. Lon felt like he was descending into the pit of hell.
But there was something there that kept him going –
he did not think of turning back.

He began to think about what he had to do. To kill a
man was a simple thing in Virginia City. Boot Hill was
already overstocked and the undertakers working
double-time. Cynical speculation did not weaken his
resolve.

The clock above the big livery-stables told him it
was ten forty-five. He passed beneath it and hitched
his horse to the tie-rail outside The Venus.

The place was half-empty. There was nobody he
knew, even by sight, except Jamie, the barman. A few
curious glances were shot at him.

'Mornin', friend,' said Jamie as he served him with
rye.

Lon figured that here was his chance to pass the
word in the time-honoured way. He said: 'Have you
seen Joe Epworth around this mornin'?'

'No, I ain't, friend. He don't usually come in till
almost noon.'

'Will you tell him the gentleman he met at the
Palace last night is looking for him?'

The words were, in themselves, innocuous, but the
sombre way in which they were spoken made the

71

barman raise his evebrows slightly. The meaning
dawned on Jamie slowly, the black look in the dark sloe
eyes before him completed the picture.

'I'll tell him,' he said. 'Yeh, I'll tell him.'

'Thanks,' said Lon. He turned on his heels and
strode from the saloon.

As he mounted his horse he figured that in doing as
he had he had maybe laid himself open for a slug in the
back. But he had done it in the traditional way, and his
conscience was clear. That conscience! his lips quirked.
Anyway, if the word got around, as no doubt it would,
Epworth could do no more to save his face, than meet
him. Unless any unforeseen 'accidents' happened to
either party beforehand.

Lon figured he'd have himself a little ride. He made
for the flatter edge of town and cantered out onto the
sand, and the straw-like dusty substance which had
once been grass. He made for the line of hills he could
see through the haze – the boundaries of 'Washoe'.

As he got further away from the town he felt the sun
more strongly on his face. He felt the old yearning in
him again – to go over those hills and keep riding. To
see what lay beyond – and still beyond.

But he knew he would not keep on riding now. He
knew he would have to turn back. Back to Virginia City
– the evil and the damned. Maybe he was damned too
– damned to the cold, calculating blood and the swift
movement, the crash of gunfire and the drifting smoke,
the knowledge that yet another man had fallen before
him, that he was still supreme. Hollow victory. Many
men had tried Lon Burton, because they felt they had
to, because they thought they could do better. He had

proved them wrong, and each time the iron had cut into his soul.

One day he would not be quick enough, and another would take his place in the smoke-ridden legend. Such was the legacy of a gunfighter.

He had thought changing his name would alter things, would start him from scratch, clean. Clean! in Virginia City! That was funny.

Already circumstances had caught up with him. He had to meet a man, he would give that man his chance – 'maulies' if he needed 'em. Maybe, even, this would be the end of his trail. Somehow, he had no fear of that, so arrogant was he in his own prowess. But afterwards he knew he would be back where he started from – Lon Burton or Hank Blundell, it was all the same. And riding to hell and back would not change things one jot.

His face was grim, his sloe eyes bleakly fixed on the hills. Distant but getting nearer. With a suddenly savage gesture he kneed his horse to a gallop. He would ride to the foot-hills then turn back. After that things could take their course.

The ride was exhilarating, the pounding of hoofs, the rhythm of the horse's stride, the sun in his eyes and the breeze in his face. When he saw the girl some of the bile lead been washed out of him, and he veered his mount and rode straight towards her.

He had recognized her immediately as the sun glinted on the golden mane of her hair beneath the wide-brimmed hat she wore. She was the same girl he had danced with last night – yet she was different in her cowgirl costume, sitting the beautiful white horse she rode as if she was part of him.

73

She turned her head as he approached, her hair wind-swept, her face like a cameo brooch he had once seen on the breast of an English duchess in San Antonio. He thought she recognized him, for he saw the flash of her white teeth; then she was leaning over the horse's neck and setting him at a gallop. He felt admiration surge within him. She was a perfect horsewoman.

He could not be at loggerheads with a gel who rode a horse like she did. He had treated her badly last night. He would show her he could do other things besides drink and fight. Oakie had said she had called the pistol-swinging Epworth off'n him. She hadn't *had* to do that. She owed him nothing. He must thank her.

These thoughts sped through his head to the rhythm of the hammering hoofs. He urged his horse to its utmost and very gradually, began to shorten the distance between them. It did not seem to him that she was running away. If she was, why make for the hills instead of the other direction? Either way he must catch her – put things right between her and him.

She threw a fleeting glance over her shoulder, but he did not catch her expression. He grinned, he was catching her now, he was catching her fast.

'Get on, boy,' he said, and the horse gave a magnificent burst of speed and drew level.

The girl turned and looked; with a jerk on the reins she slackened off her horse.

Lon lifted his hat. 'That was a good race, ma'am,' he said and smiled.

For a moment her face seemed disapproving, and his heart sank. Then suddenly she smiled too – then,

74

wonder of wonder, arched her throat and gave a little ripple of laughter.

'It was a good race,' she said. 'You ride almost as good as you fight.'

'I'm sorry about last night, ma'am,' he said. 'I was drunk I guess. An' I'd been pushed around. I don't like bein' pushed around.'

'I gathered that much,' she said.

'I haven't been used to havin' to get special invites for hoofin' parties or havin' a gink try an' stop me with a gun when I try to get in.'

'You got in.'

'Yes. I got in.' Lon grinned. 'Then look what happened.'

'That was none of my doing. I'm afraid my uncle is a hard man. He's had to be.'

'Your uncle?'

'Cyril Carpenter is my mother's brother. I haven't seen him since I was a child. I had a sudden invitation fron him, and as I very much wanted to see that Eldorado of the West, Virginia City, I accepted it.'

'And what do you think of this Eldorado?'

'It exceeds all my expectations.'

He did not ask her what she thought of her uncle, or of her new-found aunt Blanche Delacroix. He was content to know that she was not the frigid beauty he had thought her to be. And neither was she cheap! No bejewelled doxie in Washoe had that poise, that naturalness, that understanding . . . And, strangest of all, she rode a horse like she had been born on one and wore her serviceable cowgirl costume as if she had spent all her life on the windswept ranches of the Southwest.

75

He said: 'Where do you hail from, Miss – er . . .'

'The name is Dale. Katherine Dale. I come from Milwaukee. We – that is mother, father and my younger brother, Tom, have been there nine years. I was brought up on a ranch on the outskirts of Tulsa, in Oklahoma. That territory is all oil-fields now and my father hates it.' She paused, looking at him. 'You don't belong to this part of the country,' she said. 'You aren't a miner.'

'I'm just a saddle tramp,' he told her. 'I ain't got no real home I guess but I hailed first off from the Pecos in Texas. I only moseyed into Virginia City last night – about an hour-and-a-half before I met you.'

Again that little gurgle of laughter; and she said: 'You certainly lost no time in trying to crack the town wide-open.'

He grinned ruefully. 'It's a mighty tough town to try and do that to, Miss Dale.'

'Your name is, if I remember, Mr Hank . . .' She paused, her mouth a little open. He suddenly felt an almost overwhelming desire to grab hold of her, to kiss those parted lips. He drew away a little: seeing her face flush he knew she had seen that desire in his eyes.

'Blundell,' he said quickly. 'Hank Blundell.'

'You're quite a pleasant young man when you're not drunk,' she said with a little gurgle of laughter. Her flush had died. In her voice there was something of the directness of her western heritage – but it was flavoured with the coquetry of the 'civilized' East. It jarred a little on the cowboy but made him want to kiss her more than ever. Probably an Eastern-educated filly was used to being kissed quite often.

Maybe she divined his intention. Her face was faintly flushed with an overall pink once more as she turned her horse's head away from him. She said:

'I've been here almost a week. Every morning I have had my ride out to the hills and back, away from the fumes and dust of that horrible town . . . I – I feel sorry for the people who have to work there. I can't understand Uncle Cy living right on top of it like he does.'

'It's near his business.'

'Yes,' she said softly. 'And his business is his life.' Her voice rose as she added abruptly: 'I'm riding back to town now.'

He turned his horse too and rode beside her. He said: 'It's rather dangerous for a young lady like you to be out all alone. What does your uncle say about it?'

'He makes weak sounds – and returns to his mine. Don't worry, Mister Hank, I can take care of myself.' She reached suddenly into her short plaid jacket and brought forth a pearl-handled thirty-eight. 'Pretty, isn't it? It isn't only for ornament. I know how to use it.'

Lon stared at this amazing girl from back East. Was this the lily of the ball? He had an idea his mouth was hanging open. He closed it quickly like a trap.

The girl smiled sweetly and put her gun away.

Words tumbled out of his mouth before he could stop them. 'Would you have pulled that gun if I had kissed you?'

She put her head on one side and assumed a look of intense gravity. 'I don't know,' she said. 'Anyway, on horseback in the middle of the open plains is hardly the place to be kissing.'

The young man's rather sombre sloe eyes lit up; he

77

threw back his head and the strong muscles in his brown throat throbbed as he laughed. He realized suddenly what an alien sound to him that laughter was.

The girl, still smiling, said: 'We will part here, Mister Hank. I go this way.'

'Will you be riding tomorrow?'

'Yes, I think so.'

'Maybe I'll meet you again, Miss Katherine.'

'Maybe,' was the cryptic rejoinder. Then she cantered away, began to climb the hill behind the town.

He took the main trail, leading to the bottom of the street. Low down there, that was the place for him and, suddenly, he remembered what he had to do when he got there. He realized that now he did not want to do it. But the decision had, if word had gotten round, most likely been taken right out of his hands. He tried not to think about it, to take what came. He must not let a meeting with a mere girl throw him off-balance. He must be ice-cold.

At the edge of the town was a little cantina called Gonzales' Place, kept by a little Mexican who was a long way from home. As soon as he saw it, smelled the spicy familiar warm smell of it, he realized how damned hungry he was.

He entered the place and ordered a quick meal of braised steak and *frijoles*. Gonzales beamed all over his fat face to hear the soft Texas drawl once more. Lon was abrupt but, before he left, he promised to call again and have a chinwag with the little Mexican.

Although the food had satisfied and filled him, the friendly reception had thrown him once more all at sixes and sevens. He was sorry, and glad at the same time, that he had entered the place but knew that, as a Texan, he had to go through with whatever was placed before him in that vapoury street running up the slopes in front of him.

EIGHT

The spell of Virginia City fell over him again as he rode slowly along the cart-rutted main drag. He kept to the dead centre, letting the reins dangle in his hand. A ripple seemed to run through people in the street as they watched him pass. It miraculously cleared in front of him, bootheels thudded as more people congregated on the boardwalk. He knew what was in store for him then, and the old calm returned.

This was Virginia City. A new town, a new place. But it might just as well have been El Paso, or Abilene, or Tombstone, or any one of half-a-dozen others. There was the same dust, maybe a little thicker now, a little more pungent. There was the same sun, its heat, though filtered through a chemical haze, like a benediction on his head. There was the same subtle something in the air, a tautness as of a slightly vibrating violin-string, singing in his head, in his heart.

For the first time since he entered the street he looked around him. There were no eyes, only faces, for as he looked the eyes turned away from him, looked down the street in front of him. Down there was Larkin's hash-house. Nobody spoke. There was no

sound but the restless champing of a horse at The
Venus tie-rail, the sombre thudding of a stamping mill
from up on the slopes of the mountain, the slow thud of
the hoofs of the cowboy's horse.

Slowly the hoofbeats stopped as the cowboy reined
in his horse and dismounted. He led the horse to the
edge of the boardwalk and left him there, his reins
dangling.

Then the lean young man with the dark expressionless face and the long lank black hair walked on.

Walking slowly to the middle of the street once
more, his broad shoulders a little drooped, his hands
hanging at his sides, his strides long but a little
uneven in his high-heeled riding boots on the rutted
and pitted ground.

Down the street a door banged suddenly. Necks were
craned. Joe Epworth came out onto the boardwalk
opposite Larkin's place. He was smoking. He looked up
and down the street, then he flipped the stub of his
cigarette out before him. He stepped off the sidewalk,
turned sharply and began to walk. He did not seem to
be looking at the young man but at something above
and behind him.

To Lon he looked taller and cleaner than last night,
his face not so hard, a little strained. He wore no
jacket, and his vest swung open. There was a plain
leather belt around his waist, but Lon could see the
strap of the shoulder-holster across his chest. He felt
vague surprise. That did not seem right somehow. He
had never before fought a man who carried his gun in
that position.

Some folks said that in the hands of a competent

81

man, the shoulder draw had the inside edge on the old way. Well, he would soon find out.

As Epworth got nearer Lon realized he was not the arrogant, murderous *hombre* of the night before. The strain on his face and in his eyes was more evident. Was it tension, or was it fear? Maybe after all, now his rage had died he too had not wanted things to finish this way.

Lon felt a sudden unwonted tolerance. He watched the man's eyes: the distance was enough; he said clearly: 'How do you want it, Epworth?'

Epworth's eyes flared suddenly, his face puckered. 'There's only one way I want it,' he cried and went for his gun.

It was a shrug of his shoulders, a superhuman lunge, but his eyes had given him away that split second before.

His gun was out when the slug thudded into his chest. It was as if somebody had pushed him unawares, playfully. As he staggered he tried to level his gun. The next shot was a rolling echo of the first, and this time he felt it blossoming from his chest and filling his whole body with red-hot agony. Then numbness followed it, starting at his legs so that they gave way beneath him. He pitched forward. His body was cold all over when he hit the ground. So he died.

Lon Burton stood straddle-legged and looked around him. Smoke still curled from the gun in his hand. Nobody spoke or moved.

He turned about and went back to his horse. Oakie Jones and Jed Crample stood on the sidewalk nearby and looked at him. His eyes passed over them, but it was like he did not see anything any more. He mounted his horse, turned it, and cantered back down the street.

The street was empty, except when Shiner crossed it and looked up into Lon's face as he passed.

'Howdy, mister,' he said.

'Howdy, Shiner.' said Lon Burton. His eyes were as blank as the boy's but, somewhere in the depths of them, that same tortured light seemed to flicker too.

Gonzales looked into the Texan's face as he entered the cantina once more. Neither of them said anything. The fat old little Mexican had seen that look on men's faces many times. It grieved him to see it on that of one who, in his eyes, was still so young. The echoes of the two shots had rolled down the hill to him above the silence and shifting dust. He was glad that the young Texan had returned so soon, but he was sad at the manner of his return.

Lon Burton sat down and looked around him. For the first time since he had thumbed the hammer of his gun back there on the street, seen the dust puff from the breast of Epworth's shirt and his eyes glaze over as he fell, he became fully aware of himself, what he was doing, where he was.

He looked up at the sweating fat face of Gonzales, and he said: 'Have you got any tequila, *amigo?*'

'*Sí, señor,*' said Gonzales softly and turned away. Lon Burton looked around the cool gloomy little place, so like dozens of places he had been in along the Rio Grande. The last man had gone, after a surreptitious glance at the new arrival, gone to see what the shooting was about up there on Main. Shootings were common in Virginia City, but mostly they took place at night, so a noonday one was an item of more than usual interest.

Lon was alone in the cantina with Gonzales and his fat wife who flitted around in the shadows behind the bar with surprising quietness.

Gonzales returned with the tequila. 'Take one for yourself, *amigo*,' said Lon. 'Sit down with me.'

'I am honoured, *señor*,' said Gonzales with a return to a rather rusty old-world courtesy he had not used of late.

He went back to the bar and poured himself a glass of tequila. This was his own private stock – nobody bought it from him nowadays, and although he waxed prosperous he often wished he was back in his native Mexico where, though there was heat and stink and flies, things grew and men were kind and human.

He 'shooed' his wife, and she vanished into the back place. He took his drink across to the table and sat down before the tall lean Texan.

'What part of Mexico do you hail from, *amigo*?' said Lon.

Gonzales told him. It seemed that the young man knew that territory well. They talked of it and of others. Like Gonzales, the Texan had travelled much, too much for one so young, thought the philosophic Mexican. They were two birds of dubious omen, come to rest under the evil spell of Virginia City, both hoping, nevertheless, to return ultimately to their home-places. The old Mexican to die. The young Texan – who knows?

84

As they talked the murmuring of the town became normal again, the warble of Washoe, and the steady pulse above it of the stamping mills.

In his talk with the philosophic old Mexican, which lasted until dusk was falling, and brooded over the dregs of numberless glasses of tequila, Lon Burton washed away the last vestiges of his hate. Another man was dead – what has to be will be. It *had* been – to hate afterwards without knowing the reason except that the hate was somewhere mixed up in the self-thoughts of the hater, was a bad thing.

Lon Burton had another meal before he left the cantina, and, as he ate, watched the evening customers stream in. They looked at him and looked away. He had won his spurs in Washoe. He had won the right to be noticed – and to be killed on the street maybe, as he had killed Joe Epworth. He would be talked about for days because he had been faster than Joe Epworth – who had been very fast. Until the time came, maybe, when somebody who had not watched the fight disbelieved those tales – and decided to do something about that disbelief . . . .

Lon Burton rose from the table, went outside, mounted his horse and rode up the street. He dismounted outside The Venus and led his horse along the alley to the stables. The stable-lad blinked at him, was very polite, very willing.

Lon went into the saloon. He looked about him as he entered. There was a sudden almost imperceptible hush, then the babble continued. Right afterwards the band started up and the barker began to call the steps. Life went on with bawdy usualness in The Venus Bar.

85

Lon crossed to the bar. He had a bellyful of tequila but figured one shot of red-eye wouldn't hurt him none. As he was drinking it he saw Oakie Jones, playing poker with three other men at a nearby table. Jed Crample was nowhere to be seen, which seemed a mite unusual. Oakie raised his glass and nodded. Lon nodded in return. Then he crossed to the faro layout which was presided over by Lulu Sanclaire.

This time she did not greet him although he nodded and smiled in her direction. The Creole and the tall thin-moustached gambler were in attendance with her. They both gave Lon more than keen glances. He placed his bets.

He played off and on all the rest of the night and lost steadily. He knew he was in for a run of bad luck – some hint of old cowboy superstitions entered his mind – and for a moment he felt something akin to panic. But he forced it away and continued foolishly to plunge. By the time Lulu closed the bank he was broke except for a few dollars. The girl took off her green eyeshade. It was dangling in her hand as she passed him. She looked at him then, and a faint mocking smile flitted across her face.

As he watched her gracefully climbing the stairs suspicion entered his mind. Had the layout been specially 'rigged' tonight, rigged so that even he did not spot it? Rigged so that he would lose above all and be paid back for his impertinent behaviour of last night? Was that the meaning of the dark maddening woman's enigmatic smile?

He crossed to the bar and had another drink. He noted that Oakie was still playing poker and that now

Jed had a seat beside him. The monkey-faced man grinned at Lon. Oakie did not look up from his game.

Lon made for the door as Lulu Sanclaire, dressed in her red wrap, came down the stairs. He was standing in the shadows of the sidewalk, lighting a cigarette when she came through the doors. She paused on the steps, looking up and down the street, tapped one small foot impatiently – thump-thump on the hollow boards.

Lon came out of the shadows. At his footsteps she turned and looked at him. He said:

'So your conveyance has not yet arrived, Miss Sanclaire?'

'It appears not,' she said shortly.

'Perhaps I could get another one from the stables. Or a hoss maybe.' There was gentle irony in his voice.

She lifted her long skirts daintily as she went down the steps. 'Thank you,' she said. 'I'll walk.'

He fell into step beside her. 'It ain't the place to walk alone,' he said. 'Particularly if those jewels you're wearing are real.'

'They are,' she said. 'But I'll be all right – nobody would dare accost me.'

Her manner and her talk were very high-falutin to say the least, but it did not disguise that harsh timbre in her voice. Like that in the brassy voices of the percentage girls and those frilled-up scented women who passed them in the street. That brassiness behind her sultry beauty was what, despite himself, intrigued Lon Burton most of all. She was a woman of the saloons who did not act like one.

She flounced along the cart-ruts and potholes, swaying her hips, her chin held high. She did not send him away but he figured that was because she did not want to create a scene in the street.

He did not know what perverseness had made him follow her, except that maybe he had a forlorn hope of hearing the truth about tonight's faro layout, but he knew that she could have a scene if she wanted one. In spades! Gonzales' peaceful philosophy had washed away from him during his sojourn in the saloon, and he was raw again.

The girl stumbled in a pothole. He caught hold of her arm to prevent her from falling. She got on even keel then shook herself free. The abrupt slighting gesture irritated Lon.

He felt like grabbing hold of her and shaking her. Who did she think she was? With difficulty he swallowed his bile and tried to make his voice jocular as he said:

'Your driver must've gotten drunk an' be sleepin' it off someplace.'

'That's possible,' she said shortly.

They were climbing the steeper slope to the homes of the hoi-poloi. He wondered if she hung out in one of these mansions, palatial by Washoe standards. If so, running a faro layout, even in a bawdy saloon like The Venus, sure must be a profitable occupation.

He said: 'You sure gave me a beatin' tonight. I guess that puts us square, uh?'

'Faro is a game of chance,' she said.

'Yeh,' he burst out, 'Like last night.'

She turned and looked straight at him for the first time since they began to walk. She began to slow down, opposite one of the biggest houses in the whole block.

'I told you,' she said. 'Monty was careless. He likes a big percentage—' She stopped as if words had failed her. She turned abruptly and made for the big white gates opposite.

Lon growled deep in his throat like a dog with his hackles rising. He started after her. She was at the gate when he caught up with her and grabbed her arm. He swung her around. Her dark eyes were wide as she looked up into his face. She seemed to go suddenly limp. He had the bit between his teeth. His voice grated as he said:

'Where do you get this high-hat business, uh? What are yuh? Just a filly runnin' a crooked faro layout.'

He pulled her closer. She was about to say something when his mouth closed over hers. She was still limp for a second, her lips warm and soft. Then she pulled her face away. He still held her, her head on his shoulder.

Into his ear she whispered harshly: 'And what are you? Just a hired killer!'

She tore away from him then like a wildcat and ran through the wide gate, up the drive into the darkness. He stood for a moment looking at the place where she had been, his shoulders drooping as if he had been lashed with a whip.

Finally he squared them, turned abruptly on his heels and went back down the street.

NINE

He was going along the alley to the stables when he heard the movements in the blackness around him, and his hand sped to his gun. His arms were pinioned from behind. A gun was jabbed into his ribs. A voice said:

'Move forward slowly – quietly.'

Vague shapes were all about him. About four of them he figured. His hip felt light as his gun was taken. The grip was taken from his arm as he walked. With a gun pressed into his back and another one glinting in the fist of a man beside him, he could do nothing else.

They passed into the glow from the stables, but the men got behind him so that he could not see them.

'If you turn around I'll slug yuh,' growled a voice that Lon did not recognize.

The stable door swung wider and the frightened white face of the lad looked out.

'Get in there. Shut that door,' growled the man. 'Mind your own business and keep your trap shut.'

The boy disappeared and the door rattled to. 'Keep movin',' growled the man, and Lon moved around the side of the stables. A chill breeze fanned his face as they moved along the back of the town.

He stopped. 'What's the game?' he said.

He winced as the gun-barrel was jabbed cruelly into his spine. 'Keep movin' I said.'

They were around him in the gloom, moving with him, but it was too dark for him to see their faces.

Then the gun was suddenly removed from his back, and the gruff voice said: 'This'll do.'

The note of it warned Lon. He whirled desperately. The gun-barrel caught him on the crown of his head, crumpling his hat over his eyes.

As he went down he heard a voice say: 'Easy.'

He rose to his knees, shaking his head from side to side. They were all around him. They began to close in. He rose and dived at the nearest, his fists swinging. His right connected, the blow jarring all the way to his elbow. He felt exultation as the man went down. He righted himself and sprang for an outlet.

He went sprawling over an outstretched foot but rolled clear as the foot swung at him again. When he got up his way was blocked again. He turned round. He was hemmed in. The man he had struck was climbing to his feet. 'Throw him this way,' he said.

The four other men sprang together. Now he knew there were five of them. The odds were too much. He dodged desperately, flinging blows right and left, using his feet too. He felt the toe of his boot jar on bone, his knuckles scrape flesh. Then he was grabbed and thrown staggering, forward blows falling on him from all sides. His arms were pinned from behind and a man loomed up in front of him. It was the one he had knocked down, out for his revenge.

Lon kicked out. The man jumped back and cursed. Lon was flung forward by those behind, and the swinging fists of the cursing man caught him two terrific blows in the face. He went down, hitting the ground hard. They stood away from him.

He rose slowly, looking around him like a cornered animal. There was no loophole. He felt blinding rage well up inside him. He sprang to his feet and lashed out. His attack was so swift and ferocious that he had a man down and was leaping over him before the rest of them came to their senses.

He turned and struck out tigerishly at another man who dived to intercept him. His fists connected and the man wilted. Another one advanced, and his swinging fist crashed into Lon's already damaged ear. The world, shot with white lights, began to spin around him. He tried hard not to fall as the lights faded and a black pit yawned.

They were all over him, smothering him. Then their blows, agonizing, brought a measure of consciousness. He threshed and tried to strike out but was held.

Hot breath fell on his face. A voice said: 'Listen to me! Get out of town. If you don't, the next time we catch you you'll be swung from a limb. You'll find your hoss tied to an old tree a few yards away. Get out of town and stay out.'

'Let me have him,' said another voice. A vague face moved away from him. Another one took its place. A knee was ground into his stomach. He tried to dodge a swinging fist, but it exploded between his eyes. That was the last he knew.

92

He came to slowly, delicious warmth all around him, soothing his sore body and aching bones. He opened his eyes and light dazzled them so that he shut them again. He felt soft sheets with his hands. He opened his eyes, averting them from the glare of the light. The sheets were white, and part of them was covered by a slush red satin counterpane.

He squinted his eyes against the light and looked about him. He was in a square, high, panelled room with pink drapes drawn across one window, large gold framed paintings on the walls, lots of heavy expensive mahogany furniture. The bed he lay in was a mahogany four-poster with curtains to match the red satin of the bedspread. He lay weakly in the centre of its immensity. The light that blazed down upon him came from a cluster of small lanterns tricked up in a huge crystal chandelier with droppers like huge earrings.

He looked at his hands. They were bruised but clean. He ran one of them over his face. That felt hacked up somewhat, but it was dry. It seemed some-body had been having a shot at cleaning him up while he was in dreamland.

What he needed really, he thought ruefully, was a new head. It felt as big as two and had a horde of angry hornets buzzing around in it. They deafened him and made it impossible for him to think. This was all like some kind of a sick cowboy's dream – brought about by too much riding and sleeping on hard cold ground.

It seemed to him that the hornets broke away from his head and began to buzz around the room. There was so many of them that they obscured the light.

93

Everything became hazy with them. But their humming became softer and softer. All was warmth, and he slept.

When he awoke the first thing he realized was the perfume. Then he looked up into a face framed by jetblack hair. Dark eyes looked into his, and the soft voice with the harsh timbre said:

'We meet again, Killer.'

He grabbed out for her, but she eluded him. He sat up in the bed. He said:

'So this is *your* place.'

She stood at the side of the bed, just out of his reach, and said: 'It is.'

She wore a long silken gown with buttons all down the front, and a high neck. It was of a pale mauve colour and intensified her dark beauty. That little mocking smile was on her face again.

He said: 'How did I get here?'

'Shiner found you lying at the back of the house. He came and woke us and we, that is two of the men, fetched you in, cleaned you up a bit and put you to bed.'

'Where's Shiner?'

'He ran away. What happened to you? Who did this?'

He told her all he knew, answering her questions mechanically. He was still a little dazed. Under her spell too, despite what she had called him.

After he had finished she said: 'Are you going to leave Virginia City?'

'I don't like being pushed around,' was his only answer.

She shrugged. 'It's a hard town to beat, Mister Texan,' she said.

94

'You know I'm a Texan?'

'Who doesn't? I don't know what you call yourself.'

He told her. 'Thank you for having me here,' he said.

'I'd do the same for a dog.' She was trying to insult him, but her voice lacked conviction.

'I don't think you would,' he said. 'What are you standing over there for? Come closer.'

The positions were reversed. Suddenly he had the power. She moved closer. He reached out and caught hold of her hand. He said: 'I guess you an' I kinda got off on the wrong foot, Lulu. By rights we should have got on like a house on fire. We're two of a kind – you know that, don't you?' She nodded her head slowly, as if mesmerized. 'We oughta start afresh.' He began to draw her closer.

She came willingly and suddenly her resistance broke altogether. She put her arms around his shoulders, held him tightly, kissed him. She kept on kissing him all over his face, murmuring with pity at its bruises and cuts, whispering husky endearments.

It was a few minutes before he realized she was calling him 'Killer' again. The word echoed inside of him, bringing a queer pain. There was something cheap about her – was it because he had killed men, one of them only today, that she was this way about him?

Almost unconsciously he began to resist her. Her eyes were wide and a little glazed as he looked into them. She tried to cling to him. His mercurial temperament had changed once more. He said: 'Where are my clothes? I've got to get out of here.'

'You're going away?'

'Maybe.'

'You're in no shape—'

'Where are my clothes?' She winced as his grip tightened on her arms. 'They're over there in the wardrobe,' she said sullenly.

Then she flung herself on him again, asking him not to go away, she wanted him to stay – wanted him. Her frigidity had been just a shell, a pose, she wanted him.

He'd asked for it, he thought cynically. Wal, he'd got it! And with the almost-revulsion struggled a queer tenderness.

He found himself kissing her again, that dark harsh something about her calling to something inside of him, the something that was already a part of the half-evil that was Virginia City, that spell which would not leave him.

He heard the door open and pushed her away from him. An old man stood there; white hair, straggly goatee sidewhiskers that went out with the war. In his hand he held an old Peacemaker Colt. He said:

'Get him out of here. I'll give you ten minutes.'

He vanished then, and Lon said: 'Your father seems mighty angry. I want no fight with old men. Get me my clothes.'

Lulu said nothing. She went across to the wardrobe, opened it, took out his clothes one by one. She folded them hurriedly and carried them in a pile to the bed. She placed them on the satin counterpane. Then she leaned nearer.

She said breathlessly: 'You'll come back. You'll come back.' She flung her arms around him suddenly. There was sudden fury in her passion. Her lips were hot. 'Please come back,' she whispered.

96

RED SILVER!

Then she turned and ran across the room. The door banged behind her.

Lon dressed himself in a half-daze. He did not know what to make of things, and his face and body hurt like hell. He found his gunbelt but no gun. A sudden spasm of blinding rage made him sick and trembling. He began to walk across the room, stumbled and went down.

He cursed weakly. What a state to be in! He remembered the shadowy figures in the gloom, the pain, the humiliation. He fought the rage which tore his body and nerves to shreds.

He conquered it and rose and tottered to the door. It opened. Lulu's driver with his cow-face and simple expression stood there. Lon swung at him instinctively. He caught his arms and pinioned them. 'Easy, suh,' he said. 'Miss Lulu says—'

'Take me to the door,' said Lon. 'I'll find my own way.'

The man let him go. 'Yes, suh. This way.'

He led Lon out back. The cowboy cursed and waved him away. The man went back into the house. Lon stood teetering, the night breeze on his face.

He stumbled around until he found his horse, tied to a tree just as the gruff-voiced man had said it would be. He climbed laboriously into the saddle and urged the beast down the slopes behind Virginia City.

When Gonzales went out back of his cantina the following morning to feed his small string of horses he found his young Texan *amigo* asleep in the barn, his bruised face staring whitely upwards, a ridge of muscle around his jaws, which were as tight as a trap.

97

The cowboy awoke, alert in an instant. He jerked upwards, and as his hand reached to his belt, his face puckered involuntarily with pain.

'Tees all right, keed,' said Gonzales. He went back to the stable door and called his buxom wife. Between them they helped the cowboy back into the house. By the time he reached there his stiffness had gone a little, and he was able to walk himself.

Mrs Gonzales plied him with hot black coffee laced with rum, then gave him ham and eggs, beans and flapjacks dripping with syrup.

After that he smoked a couple of long black cheroots with enough kicks in them to singe a man's ear off. He told his tale, as much as he knew, and omitting a few details on his own account. Gonzales was indignant but could offer no clues.

'You're one tough *hombre*,' he said.

'Warn't no more than ridin' wild hosses,' said Lon. He was his old cocky self once more. But there was an added grimness underlying it all.

'Can I lay up here for a short while, oldtimer? Upstairs mebbe where nobody can see me – an' nobody to be told.'

'For sure, *amigo*. Trust us.'

TEN

The boy at the stables behind The Venus Bar was called Hanky. He was a slight pale-faced youth of timid nature. The origin of his nickname was unknown. He had arrived in Virginia City a year ago with his uncle, who was a professional gambler. He was Hanky then. While his uncle manipulated the pasteboards in the saloon the boy spent most of his time with the horses. He seemed to have a way with them. Then his uncle got killed in a gunfight, and he was left destitute. Shortly afterwards the Mexican stableman high-tailed it with a woman of the town who was somebody else's wife. Hanky, who had stuck closer to the place than a burr on a buffalo's hide just naturally fell into the job. He had been on it ever since.

He saw a lot, heard a lot and often feared a lot. He had learnt to keep his mouth shut. But he was at a romantic and idealistic age, prone to glorious daydreams and spasms of hero worship. He had heard of the tall Texan's exploits in the saloon and dance-hall on his first night in town. Texas was a golden word to the boy who came from back East. It was the land of Hickok and Earp and O'Niel and Texas Bill. It was the golden land. The tall lean dark ranny with the catlike walk and the lowslung gun was one of its sons and a worthy one. Hanky, from the shelter of the alley, saw the young man kill the fast-shooting Joe Epworth, and he was filled with a trembling awe.

The same night he saw his idol driven up the alley at the point of a gun to vanish into the darkness behind surrounded by hardfaced men. Men who the boy knew and feared for their ruthlessness.

Because he feared them he held his peace, and the lean Texan vanished from his ken.

Hanky was sorely troubled. Consequently it was a relief as well as a surprise when, a couple of nights later, his idol appeared once more, whole again and grimmer than ever. He came silently on foot from around the back of the stable. He wanted some information.

All Hanky's old fears returned. He hedged; he had not seen the men properly, he had gone back into the stables as soon as they threatened him, he had not recognized their voices.

'Wouldn't you like to see the town free from folks like that, son?' said the man.

Hanky nodded his head mutely, gabbled on. 'I don't know anythin', mister – honest—'

The cowboy's eyes suddenly blazed. He reached out and grasped the boy's shoulders. 'I've got just so much patience, son – an' it's runnin' out.' He shook the trembling Hanky.

Footsteps sounded in the alley, and he let him go. He went through the door. The man who approached stared curiously after his retreating back.

'Who was that?' he said.

'I dunno,' said Hanky. 'He's a stranger to me.'

The man took his horse and went. But others were on the way; their bootheels thudded nearer. From the shadows a voice hissed:

'I'll be at Gonzales' place if you want to see me, son. Don't be scared – I'll look after you.'

The boy went to the door and looked out into the empty blackness. Then he turned to greet the next half-drunken arrivals who were clamouring for their cayuses.

When Lon Burton left the stable, he went right back to the cantina. He sat in his upstairs room and composed himself to wait although he felt like going down there and shooting up the town. It was probable that his wait would be in vain. If so he would have to think of another angle. For a moment he felt rage against the vacillating stable-boy. He killed it: maybe the kid would turn up trumps after all. He decided to wait a little longer then go back there.

To while away the time he took out his gun and oiled it and checked it. It was a Frontier model Colt he had borrowed from Gonzales. His own gun was still missing. Maybe it would turn up again – in somebody else's belt. Whoever carried it would figure that the Texan had high-tailed it. If Lon caught the galoot! – there were possibilities in that angle too. He sifted them around in his mind for a while. As he waited his thoughts became more savage.

He was jerked erect by the sound of somebody hammering furiously on the back door, a voice yelling unintelligible words. He heard Gonzales shouting in

101

return. The voice rose almost to a scream. Gonzales shouted: 'Hank! Hank *amigo*.'

The Texan took the stairs two at a time. Gonzales was just beginning to climb them. He was wringing his hands, his fat face glistening with sweat.

His babblings were incoherent for a moment. Lon quietened him down to learn that the commotion had been caused by Shiner. Murder was being done. Outside a man lay dying.

'Where is Shiner?'

'He ran off, Hank. I could not stop him. Where he go I don't know.' Gonzales began to wring his hands once more.

'Pull yourself together oldtimer,' said Lon. 'Let's see who's out there. Come on.'

He whipped past the old man, who shuffled after him as he ran through the kitchen. His wife turned wide-eyed from the back door.

'I thought I saw something,' she said. 'Out there by the rocks.' She pointed, backing fearfully.

Lon drew his Colt. He went through the door at a stooping run, flung himself into the shadows out of the path of light. Nothing happened.

He crouched there for a moment, his eyes raking the darkness. Then he ran towards the cluster of rocks. He went down beside the body lying face downwards.

He touched the frail back, and his fingers came away sticky. A sudden feeling of unbearable pity and sadness almost choked him as he turned the body over. His hand was trembling as he felt inside the worn leather jacket. There was no flicker of life there.

Lon rubbed his wet hands in the sand. He was trem-

102

bling all over. He would never know what Hanky had meant to tell him. The poor kid was cut to ribbons.

He did not know how long he knelt by the body, thinking of the promise he had made to look after the kid, and how miserably he had failed. He was brought to his senses by Gonzales calling his name softly.

He rose. It was then, on top of the old Mexican's sibilant tones he heard the horse's nicker. He whirled, drawing his gun once more. His eyes tried to pierce the darkness. He advanced slowly.

He saw the horses, a whole string of them. They were tied together with rawhide and had no saddles. He was trying to make something out of this new puzzle when Gonzales joined him.

'The boy,' the little fat man said. 'Why would anybody want to kill the boy?'

Lon did not answer. He jerked his thumb. 'What d'yuh make o' this?'

Gonzales was silent for a moment. Then he said:

'I guess they are mine – Shiner was bringing them for me.' He looked around him as if he expected the simple big-eyed youth to materialize from the gloom. 'Where is he? Where has he gone?'

'I think maybe I know,' Lon said. Then he spoke decisively. 'Take these horses into the stables, old one. I will bring the body.'

Carrying what remained of Hanky was like carrying a child. He laid him on the couch in the Gonzales kitchen and covered him with a blanket. Then he turned and made his request.

'Don't tell anybody about this. I'm going out, but I hope to come back soon. If Shiner should happen to come back keep him here.'

'We will do as you say, Hank,' said Gonzales.

The young man went out and got his horse and rode up the hill once more. Into the darkness behind the town – although its glow was in the sky above him; its stink and its noise came to him like the pulsing of a monstrous heart.

He was climbing steeply when he turned into an alley. When he came out the other side he was among the mansions of the rich. He was shunning conceal-ment now, but his reasons for doing so were obscure even to himself.

The carriages were taking home the mighty after their night of enjoyment. Lon's thoughts were bitter as he watched them rolling by. They had built their pros-perity on the blood and sweat of such as Hanky, who lay dead down there at the bottom of the hill. God, somebody would have to pay – somebody would have to pay dearly!

A familiar black and gold carriage went past. A pale cameo-like face looked from a window. Lon bowed iron-ically and took off his hat. The face looked out at him frigidly and then turned away. Could you beat that? These damn women – they were more unpredictable than the wind over the Rio Grande.

A horrible suspicion suddenly clouded his mind, another doubt added to all the others. He was wrestling with it as he urged his horse up the steep hill and veered into the darkness.

He was challenged, and he reined in his mount and waited. Oakie Jones came out of the darkness.

'Jumpin' fish,' he said. 'Hank. I thought you'd lit out for good.'

Jed joined them, and his astonishment was as great.
Lon noted however that neither of them holstered their
guns. He took a chance, a very big chance for him to
whom a gun was a third arm – he took out his Colt and
handed it over. 'I came in peace,' he said.

All his life he had been a gambler as well as a
fighter. He was playing long odds now, but he did not
hesitate.

Oakie took the gun and tucked it into his belt.

'Light down, Hank,' he said. 'An' come into the
parlour.'

'Said the spider to the fly,' quoted 'Hank'. His voice
was humourless. He followed the two men, who both
holstered their guns.

Jed dropped back, took the reins out of his hands. He
led the horse over to the stables.

Oakie ushered the young Texan into the living-cabin
with the incongruous old furniture. Then he turned
and faced him.

'You wouldn't be looking for Shiner by any chance,
Would you?' he asked.

'Yes, I'm looking for him. How did you know?'

Oakie shrugged. 'Just a long shot. He's up the back
someplace. We stopped him on his way up. He babbled
somep'n about a murder then he skedaddled. We could-
n't stop him. Do you know anythin' about it, Hank?
Whose murder?'

The young man told him. Oakie said: 'Mebbe Shiner
saw who did it – that's why he's so scared.'

'That's what I figured. We'd better go after him.' He
turned.

'Hold it, son,' said Oakie. 'We'll never catch Shiner if

we go crashin' up there after him right now. I know
Shiner. When he's scared he's like an animal. What I
vote we do is sit back an' wait for him. He'll come back
when he's cooled down a bit. He knows no harm'll come
to him here so I figure this is the place he'll make for.'

'Mebbe you're right,' said Lon dully. He was looking
at the two guns in Oakie's belt.

The big man interpreted his gaze. He took out the
Frontier model Colt and handed it over butt foremost.
Lon sheathed it.

The two men measured glances. Something struggled in their eyes, an attempt to understand each other
fully. Oakie said:

'Sit down, Hank. Tell me what you've been doing
with yourself these last few days.'

Jed entered, a curious look on his monkey-face. Lon
sat down and unburdened himself. He missed nothing
out. He wondered if the two men had heard any of it
before.

He did not tell them about Lulu's lovesick behaviour, only of her saving of him and the appearance of
her hornery old father. Jed sniggered. Oakie said:

'Ol' coot with a goatee an' side-frills?'

'Yep, that's him.'

'That ain't Lulu's father. That's her husband.'

'Her husband?'

'Yeh, Pop Quail, one of the first mine owners here.
Lulu hooked him jest after he made his big
bonanza—'

'But The Venus. Her set-up there—?'

'That's what she did before – that an' other things.
She left it for a bit – then I guess she got tired of her

gilded cage an' moved back. She likes plenty o' life does Lulu – an' Pop ain't got much left. She'll be sitting pretty when he cashes in his chips.'

Lon Burton did not say anything. That blinding rage was surging in him once more. He tried to control it, hoped it did not show in his face.

'It's kind of a hard thing to hear about the gel, ain't it, Hank?' said Oakie.

'Yeh, I guess so. But who are we to judge?' Lon was surprised at the levelness of his own voice. He went on with his tale.

When he told them about the string of hosses he found after the murder and Shiner's flight Oakie interrupted again, saying: 'I had an idea that was where the little skunk was taking 'em.'

'What's that?'

The hosses that Shiner stole. He's bin selling 'em to Gonzales. He must have been taking that string up there when he saw the killing.' Oakie snapped his fingers. 'It's a perfect set-up. Gonzales' place is right on the edge of town. Any stranger could get in an' get away again without bein' seen – particularly at night. The way you managed to hole up there proves that. I'm beginning to think that Shiner, even if he is a scairy-cat, ain't quite so crazy as he seems. An' I guess you cain't exactly blame Gonzales. Everybody is on the make in this fair city.'

'The old fox,' sad Lon Burton. Then he looked at Oakie sharply. 'If Shiner did see the killing like you said – an' didn't jest find the body – mebbe the killers saw him too. I guess that's why he ran awlright.'

Oakie's face puckered. He rose. 'I guess we'd better

go out an' have a looksee,' he said. 'He may be comin' down now.'

The phlegmatic Jed was nearest the door. He opened it, stepped out into the darkness.

The other two heard him say 'hey', then the rest of his words were drowned in a blatter of shots. They died. There was a queer choking sound.

Jed came slowly back into the cabin. The choking sounds came from his throat. There was a look of intense surprise on his puckered monkey-face. Oakie caught him as he fell; with his foot the big man kicked the door to. He lowered his pard to the floor. When he let him go his hands came away covered with blood from the rapidly spreading patch on Jed's chest. He looked at Lon. Lon drew his gun, turned swiftly and shot out the light. Both men fell flat on their stomachs as shots boomed and echoed once more. The sound died away in ghostly echoes over the mountain.

Oakie was cursing softly, terrible, under his breath. His voice had a catch in it.

A piece of glass fell suddenly with a tinkle from a broken window. 'Are you with me now, Hank,' said Oakie. 'Are you with me?'

'Yeh, I'm with yuh.'

'There's the men who killed Hanky, there's the men who beat you up. Out there, out there lookin' for Shiner – an' figurin' to wipe us out too an' clear the slate.'

'They won't do that, oldtimer. They'll never clear the slate.' Lon Burton began to move, to crawl towards the window.

As he reached it shots boomed again, glass flew and

slugs thudded into the door and the log walls. The shots seemed to be nearer.

'I guess they're closing in,' said Oakie. 'I wonder if they've got Shiner.'

Lon Burton said nothing for a bit. He was beside the window, his hat off, shoving his dark head around the corner.

Oakie wriggled across to him. Outside was an area of deep and deeper shadows. They waited for one of these shadows to move. Finally they were rewarded. They both opened up. A man cried out in agony. Then the barrage started again.

Both men dodged back. 'That was mighty careless of them,' hissed Lon Burton. His eyes glowed in the darkness as he turned towards his companion.

He went on: 'Mebbe if you kept 'em busy from here I could dodge outside.'

'It's risky, Hank.'

'Yeh, but it's better than sitting here waiting for 'em to get all around us. We don't know how many there is.'

'I figure about four.'

'Yeh, that's what I figured. An' there's one of 'em out o' the runnin' by the sound o' things. Now's the time to attack, while they're still bunched. There's a chance Shiner might still be out there too.'

Oakie loomed up straight in the darkness. 'All right, I'll go. It was my pard they killed.'

Moving catlike for all his bulk, he crossed to the door.

'Oakie—'

The big man's voice came back. 'I'll git Jed's gun an' toss it to yuh. You start shootin' – pronto.'

109

Lon shrugged. 'Awlright, pardner,' he said. He darted across to the other side of the window. 'I'll cover you from here.'

Hardly were the words out of his mouth when the attackers opened up again. Above the din Lon could hear Oakie relieving his tense feelings in curses. Then it died.

'Catch,' said Oakie. 'I'm goin'.'

Lon caught the gun which was tossed to him. He moved, swivelled, faced the window. He thumbed the hammers of both guns as fast as he could, sending hot lead screaming out into the night.

He thought he heard the door bang; he knew Oakie was outside facing them, but he was deafened by his own gun-music, blinded by the smoke and the sting of cordite.

He felt the wind of a slug at his cheek. another plucked at his shoulder. He moved away from the window, flung himself at the door, opened it. As he dived out he saw Oakie against the wall. The big man was reloading. He rose and began to advance, thumbing the hammer of his gun.

Slugs thudded into the door behind Lon. He moved aside and, half-crouching, began to walk too.

He fired at flashes in the blackness in front of him. He felt a wild exultation as out of the corner of his eye, he saw that Oakie was still moving too.

Then there were no more flashes up ahead, and he held his fire as the big man bawled:

'They're running. Goddam 'em, they're running!' He began to stumble after them and went down flat.

As Lon reached him hoofs were clattering away. He

helped the big man to his feet.

'You all right, Oakie?'

'Jest a flesh wound in my thigh. Pesky laig let me down then . . . . Goddam them! By the time we git our hosses they'll be back in their holes.'

'I think we got a couple of 'em,' said Lon. 'Over here.' He led the way.

A man was sprawling full length on his face. Lon looked around. 'He seems to be the only one,' he said. 'I'm sure we hit one or two more. They must've been able to get away.'

'Mebbe we'll spot 'em later,' said Oakie. He turned the body over. 'He's dead all right.' He got down on his knees and peered closely into the face. 'It's one of Hiram Vanberger's men.'

Lon got down beside him. He recognized those horselike features with the long scar down the one cheek. It was Hackett, the man he had slugged that night he called on his old friend Mike Hanlon – alias Hiram Vanberger. The sly little skunk.

Now the fight was over Oakie Jones's body sagged tiredly. He muttered something and turned and walked back towards the cabin. Lon started to follow him, then swung once more on his heels. He grabbed the body under its armpits.

He propped it up against the wall of the hut. He went inside, stood just over the threshold. Oakie was fumbling around, hanging blankets up at the windows. Lon joined him. They worked in silence.

Finally Oakie crossed back to the centre of the room saying: 'I guess that'll shut out the light in case they should happen to come back. They won't be able to see

111

us. Go see the door is shut. I'll light the lamp.'

Lon closed the door tight. Oakie lit the lamp, the glass of which had been smashed by Lon's shot. Garish yellow light illuminated the room with painful clarity. The dead face of Jed Crample stared piteously upwards.

ELEVEN

'Help me to lift him,' said Oakie.

They carried Jed to the bunk, laid him there and covered him up.

Oakie looked round the room aimlessly, his big hands dangling.

'Have yuh got any cawfee?' said Lon. He was the cool collected one now. All his rage had died. He could bide his time. Till hell came . . . .

Oakie nodded mechanically and jerked a thumb. Lon went through the door of the little lean-to kitchen, flung it wide. He reached up for the can of coffee on the shelf opposite. Then he froze.

There was the unmistakable sound of softly, slowly padding footsteps around the back of the cabin. The Texan lowered his hand. He turned and catfooted into the cabin and hissed a warning to Oakie. Then he crossed to the door.

He stood with his hand on the latch; and with his other one he drew his gun. The big man made a movement. Lon waved him back: he drew his gun and stood by the table and waited.

Suddenly Lon flung the door open, his gun raised.

113

There was a frightened yelp, and Shiner almost fell head-first into the room.

'Quit the play actin',' snarled Lon. 'Where've you bin?'

Shiner straightened up. His lidless eyes shone horribly in the light. 'Up on the mountain I bin,' he said. 'I heard the shootin'. I waited.'

'You saw the folks who killed Hanky didn't yuh? They came after yuh?'

'Ye-eh.'

Lon flung open the door again. He went outside. When he reappeared he was dragging the body of the scarfaced man. 'Is this one of 'em?'

Shiner peered. His eyes bulged terribly with concentration. Finally he said: 'Yeh, that's one of 'em.'

'Who else was there?'

Shiner held his hand so far above the floor. 'One was a little fellah, walked with a limp.'

'That'd be Cal Harris,' put in Oakie. 'He's a Vanberger man.'

'Who else?'

'I didn't know the others,' said Shiner.

'Who knifed Hanky?'

'Two of 'em. He was one.' He jerked his thumb at the body. 'The other was a tall thin feller.' He suddenly noticed the body of Jed. He went across to it and dropped on his knees.

'Did one of those fellers do this to Jed?'

'Yeh, he never had a chance.'

'Jed was my pard.'

He rose and turned to Lon once more. 'You our pard now – me an' Oakie's?'

114

'Yes, Shiner.'

'I ain't scared any more,' said Shiner. 'We'll go find them fellers.'

'We'll get 'em sooner or later, Shiner. There's lots o' things we gotta do. You can help us. We jest got to think things out a little first.' Lon turned to Oakie, went across to him. 'Sit down, pardner,' he said.

It was night in Virginia City – or rather early morning, which was the only time Washoe slept. The streets were promenades for prowling cats who sent their cries to the stars and the dust chittered sibilantly in the breeze beneath the boardwalks.

Three men rode up the street on the backs of padded-hoofed horses. They led two more beasts whose riders did not sit upright but sagged across bare backs. One beast had a burden of two, the other only one.

They halted finally outside the old jail which was as empty now as a tin bucket with holes in it. They relieved the two horses of their burdens and propped the three forms like rag dolls against the wall of the jail. One of the men had a white paper which he fastened to the door. The three men mounted again and, leading the two bare-backed horses, went on up the hill.

One of them dismounted halfway up there and crossed to a gate in a white picket fence before a large frame and brick house. He opened the gate and walked up the short drive. A few moments later there was the tinkle of broken glass. The man reappeared and vaulted onto his horse. Then the three of them set their mounts at a gallop.

A light flashed on in an upstairs window of the big house they had left. A little man in a voluminous night-shirt got out of bed with a revolver in his hand. He looked about him. He shivered as a cold breeze from the broken window fanned his meagre shanks. He crossed the room and picked up something from the carpet.

It was a rock with a sheet of white paper tied around it. He unfolded the paper and tossed the rock on the bed. A message was scrawled on the paper. His lips worked as he spelled out the words:

You should have forgotten your conscience and had me killed outright. You will not get another chance. – L. B.

The little man cursed, crumpled the paper into a ball and threw it on the floor. L.B. had always had a devilish sense of humour.

Virginia City began to come awake with the first glint of the sun. Dawn was too early. The first man on Main Street was an oldtimer who led a burro and a horse from a tumbledown stable. He tied the burro's leadrope to the horse's saddle-horn and forked the beast. He had a Colt in his belt, a Winchester in his saddle-boot, a quirt in one horny hand. The rest of his belongings were packed into a rolled tarp tied on the burro's back.

The oldtimer was leaving the county of Washoe for good. He had had enough of grubbing for silver – and not having a chance to mine it properly even if he found any. He was going to make his way by easy stages to Arizona. He had heard they were finding gold along the border.

He let loose a string of profanity at the lethargic burro as he passed the jail. Then he saw the three men, and he figured that was a queer place to sleep – no bedrolls either and the night waxing cold of late. He was a curious old man; he turned and cursed the burro once more and led the horse over to the tie-rail, looping the reins there. The horse snorted and backed away as far as he could go. The old man frowned in sudden alarm as he climbed onto the boardwalk. He had seen too much of death to mistake it now.

He stooped nearer to the grotesque bodies, the grotesque dead masks. He shuddered a little as he spoke names under his breath.

'Slim Hackett – Jed Crample – Hanky.' The pitiful bundle that had once been Hanky slid sideways, rolled over. The oldster looked closer and swore softly beneath his breath.

He straightened and looked around him. He was sorry that now he had found this thing he could not yet leave the town. He hated it: he cursed again, cursed the town and all who lived in it. Then he saw the white paper tacked onto the wall of the jail.

He peered at it short-sightedly, shaping letters with his lips. He regretted that he had never learned to read properly. He untied his horse. 'Come on, fellah,' he said. He started back the way he had come.

A man appeared in the street by The Venus. The oldster waved to him and shouted. His words were garbled, but something of the urgency in them was communicated to the man, distilled into the very air. The man began to run.

He drew to a skidding halt when he saw the things

117

outside the jail. Then he, too, shouted. He ran on, thudding on to the boardwalk, dancing about in front of the bodies, looking into the faces. Then he turned and ran to the edge of the boardwalk and began to yell again.

The oldtimer, anxious not to miss anything, stashed his horse and his burro and came outside again. By that time many more people were coming into the street and running towards the point of interest.

The oldtimer broke into a shuffling lopsided run himself. He hopped onto the boardwalk and through the small press. Three men were looking at the sheet of paper on the jail wall.

'What's it say?' said the oldtimer. 'What's it say?' The crowd was growing. There were murmurs of astonishment, of horror, of menace.

'Listen to this, folks,' bawled a man. The crowd became hushed as he began to read the notice:

TO THE MINERS AND CITIZENS OF VIRGINIA CITY

You see before you all that remains of Jed Crample and the boy we know as Hanky. They were good men. Can anybody say they were not? Beside them is another man who is not so good. He was a member of the gang who murdered our two friends. You all know to which gang he belonged

A murmur arose from the crowd. In some sections it rose to a shout.

'Wait a minute!' bawled the reader. 'That ain't all. Listen! This is the juicy bit.' He paused, for he had a sense of the dramatic. Then:

118

*This thing that has happened to Jed and Hanky is an example of the so-called justice of the robbers and slavers who have seen fit to call themselves bosses of this fair town of ours. Under their so-called rule Virginia City is travelling right to hell. Are you, miners and citizens, going to stand by and see this happen? Are you going to continue to be exploited and bullied in their mines in danger and semi-starvation while they sit in their big houses and count their profits and entertain their women? There will be a meeting in The Venus tonight at nine when the murderers will be denounced and a new way of life proposed for us all. Where would the profits of these murderers and robbers be if it were not for us? Take a stand now for justice and better conditions. Down tools everybody!*DON'T FORGET THE MEETING TONIGHT. THE VENUS BAR. NINE O'CLOCK

The reader's voice rose to a crescendo – then died. For a moment there was dead silence. Then somebody shouted:

'Who signed it?'

'There ain't any signature,' replied the reader.

'Whoever wrote it is a scholar who knows his onions,' said somebody else.

Talk became general then. It murmured, it rumbled; it was sullen – then it rose to a menacing crescendo. There were arguments: many suspected trickery; many of the townspeople, profit-seekers too, were openly in favour of the people who were indirecty indicted in the terms of the notice. Then the miners,

119

pale and smudge-faced from the first shift in the damp and fumes of the mines, arrived to swell the ranks. They were always spoiling for mutiny. Only a spark was needed to start the conflagration, and a leader to guide the flames in the right direction. There was the spark. Where was the leader?

Things were beginning to get out of hand, there was talk of lynching, and a loud-mouthed storekeeper was knocked down and stamped upon – and still no leader – when Lawyer Sanderson arrived on the scene.

The lawyer, who was a tall cadaverous man with a squint, had been woken up by the shindig. Being so early in the morning he was cold-sober – an unusual state for him – and peevish to boot.

He carried a derringer in each hip pocket and was frightened of nothing on earth. He elbowed his way to the front of the mob, snarling from time to time: 'What's goin' on here? What's goin' on?'

He came to a halt in front of the three bodies. He stood straddle-legged looking down at them, as if he was arraigning a jury, his hands thrust in his pockets – probably caressing his derringers – and his head jutting forward from rawboned shoulders.

'What's this? Who done this?'

'This notice, Mistuh Sanderson—'

'Hey? What's that?' He strode forward, read the notice swiftly, wagging his head.

'Humph!' he said. He turned. 'Guess we'd better have an inquest. Anybody know anythin' about this?'

Nobody seemed to. 'All right!' said the lawyer, 'Pick 'em up. Take 'em down to The Venus. We'll have an inquiry right away.'

Lawyer Sanderson liked inquests, and he invariably held them in The Venus Bar, for they had the best liquor there.

The murmuring died as men gently lifted the bodies of Jed and Hanky. The crowd parted to let them through. Virginia City still had a heart someplace – though it was kind of soiled.

The remains of Slim Hackett received rougher treatment. He was tossed over the heads of the crowd like a rag doll, and the heart of Virginia City was swamped again by inherent lust and brutality.

'Take it easy with that body,' said Lawyer Sanderson. 'I want it all in one piece.'

A roar of laughter greeted this sally. Deputies in the crowd tried their best not to look like lawmen. Law had been a mockery in Virginia City for a long time. Right now the set-up seemed on the point of blowing up in their faces. They sidled away to pass on the news. This rabble must be stopped before they really got out of hand.

The deputies wished Lawyer Sanderson in hell. That cynical fearless man could do just what he liked with that crowd. And nobody on earth could tell which way he would jump.

TWELVE

The crowd surged into The Venus. Undertaker Emmanuel Grocott pushed his way to the front and hovered around the bodies which were now laid on the table.

'Get away from there, Manny,' yelled the lawyer. 'You can have 'em when I'm finished with 'em – and not until.'

There was another roar of laughter. The lawyer took his seat on the high chair behind the bar. He had borrowed a heavy Colt from somebody. With this he hammered the bar.

'Order,' he bawled. 'We will begin the inquest.'

As silence came he shouted again. 'Are there any witnesses of how these men met their death?'

Nobody came forward. 'This is a fine state of affairs,' said the lawyer. 'Who put these bodies there?' Nobody knew that either. Sanderson vented his spleen by hammering the bar once more. 'What a bundle of gaping jackasses,' he bawled.

He got another laugh but no help from anybody. Outside voices were rising as folks tried to get into the already packed saloon. They almost filled the street as

they milled across it. There were rumours that at some
of the mines, men had already downed tools. Indeed
there seemed to be a lot of miners in the crowd.
Swedes, Italians, half-breeds; bunches of impassive-
faced Chinese labourers from the Golden Gate who, in
contrast to their loud-mouthed mates, remained silent.

A man on horseback came down the street. He was
a little man with a scowling face. Somebody in the
crowd cried: 'There's Cal Harris. He's one o' the
buzzards. He's one o' Vanberger's men.'

The stocky man's scowl became more pronounced.
He spurred his horse forward. His left wrist was
bandaged. He held the reins with his left-hand and his
other dropped to his gun.

The majority of this outside crowd were workmen.
They were loud-mouthed and truculent. But they were
used to being told what to do. They were slow to act
without orders. Those nearest to Cal Harris backed
away to let his horse pass. Those at the back could go
on with their yelling, but nobody close to the Vanberger
gunman's deadly right-hand was going to risk a quick
movement.

As Harris urged his horse forward a Chinese in a
short cotton smock got in his path. The gunman cursed
and pulled the horse onto its hind legs. A flying hoof
caught the Oriental on the shoulder, sending him spinning. Then Harris crashed through the outer ring and
rode on.

At the bottom of the hill another horseman came
into view and came slowly upwards. Somebody in the
crowd said: 'That's Oakie Jones, Jed Crample's pard.'

The distance between the two men shortened. Then

123

they were almost face to face. 'Running away, Cal?' said Oakie's deep mocking voice.

'I never run away from anythin'.'

'So be it. This is the furthest you go in this direction, Cal.'

'Get out of my way, you—' Harris spurred his horse forward, his good arm moving swiftly.

The two reports were almost simultaneous. Harris's horse broke into a frenzied gallop and raced past the other beast and his rider. Harris suddenly toppled from the saddle – but his one foot caught fast in the stirrup, and he was dragged along by the speeding horse.

Oakie Jones's Stetson rolled in the dust. He ignored it. Turning, he rode his horse at a gallop after the other racing beast.

As the crowd watched and shouted encouragement, three more horsemen appeared at the bottom of the hill. One of them rode forward and stopped the runaway mount, then dismounted and slung Cal Harris across the saddle.

The other two caught up as he remounted. The horse, with its burden amongst them, they joined Oakie. They were recognized as they came nearer. The lean young Texan who had killed Joe Epworth (folks said his name was Hank); young Shiner; and Gonzales the keeper of the cantina.

'Let us come through,' yelled Oakie Jones. 'We've got another body to add to the collection.' He indicated Cal Harris, hanging slackly like a sack of meal on the saddle.

The news spread into the saloon. 'What's going on?' bawled Lawyer Sanderson. 'Order! Order I say!' For once nobody took any notice of him, and his eyes bulged from his cadaverous face as a horseman suddenly rode full-tilt through the double doors. The rest of the assembly gaped, then staggered for cover. This was the first time anybody had entered The Venus in that manner.

The lean young man astride the horse shouted: 'Make way for my pards, folks – an' another body. All witnesses – kind of – in this case.' He had a Texan way of speaking so maybe that explained his unconventional entrance. Men recognized him and held their peace. He dismounted from his horse and the beast stood in a startled manner in the middle of the floor.

'What's going on?' said Lawyer Sanderson a little plaintively. Nobody was looking at him so he took a swig from the bottle of whiskey he had stolen from behind the bar. The wide-eyed Shiner, grinning a slack-mouthed grin because he was one of the centres of attraction, followed Lon on foot. Behind him came Gonzales and Oakie carrying the body of Cal Harris. They straightened this out on the table beside the other three.

Oakie lingered a little, looking into the dead face of his pard, Jed. 'I'm sorry we had to do it like this,' he whispered. 'But I guess you're glad to still be in on things, you ol' buzzard.'

He turned away swiftly then, following Gonzales. The young Texan handed his horse's reins to Shiner.

'Jest park him outside, boy.'

Shiner went. The other three waited until he returned then the four of them walked to the bar to confront Lawyer Sanderson.

The tall thin man regarded them owlishly. 'So you've brought me another customer have you? Who is it?'

'Another one o' the killers.'

'Can you prove that allegation?'

'We can.'

As Oakie spoke Shiner's grin widened, and he took a step forward. Lon Burton laid a cautionary hand on his arm.

'Did you park those bodies by the jail and pin up that notice?'

'We did.'

'You're a bit early for your meeting aren't you?'

'Things kinda got out of hand. But we'll still have that meeting.'

'Well, now that is settled, might I be allowed to go on with *my* meeting,' said Sanderson with crushing irony.

'You may.'

After that the proceedings went pretty smoothly. It was the nicest inquest Sanderson had ever held; everybody was so interested in the tale that was unfolded by the lean Texan, and the simple boy, and the rest of them, that nobody seemed to notice how many times the lawyer hit the bottle.

All the cards had been laid on the table, everybody was chewing the fat, and the air was thick with threats. The lawyer hammered on the bar with the butt of the Colt.

'Quiet!' bawled Oakie Jones.

Finally order was restored. 'I'll try to make my summing-up as unbiased as possible,' said Sanderson, beaming benignly upon his flock.

'After the evidence that has been brought forward

there is little doubt in my mind that there,' he pointed at the row of bodies, 'we have two murdered people and also two of the people who murdered them. As to other murderers – no proof has been brought forward. This is not a court of law – only an inquiry – so I will let the other allegations pass and leave everybody to draw their own conclusions.' He quelled a growing murmur with an uplifted hand. 'On two of the deceased I bring in a verdict of murder – by persons known and others unknown shall we say – and on the other two a verdict to the effect that they only got what they damn well asked for.'

A chorus of 'Hear, hear' and roars of laughter followed this last sally. Sanderson beamed and reached for the whisky. Then he changed his mind – right now too many folks were looking. The crowd began to mill.

'How about that meeting?' yelled somebody.

The lean young Texan jumped up onto the table. 'There'll still be a meeting,' he shouted. 'Nine o'clock like we said. I guess there ain't enough room here so it'll be outside the saloon instead of in it. Get goin' an' pass the word around. We want every miner in Washoe to be here – an' the mine owners or their representatives are welcome too if they want to come. They might as well so they can hear what's in store for 'em . . . .'

'We'll drag 'em out if they don't come,' yelled somebody.

'Take it easy,' bawled Oakie Jones. 'We want no lynch mob here. You'll never get what you want that way—'

The growling died once more. The young man on the table said: 'If there's anybody here right now who

127

thinks things shouldn't be done like we've proposed let him come forward an' say so, an' I'll try to persuade him different.' He grinned and raised his voice. 'I'm a Texan on the prod – who's with me?'

Shouts greeted his words, and the sounds rose to a roar.

The Texan bawled: 'On your way then. Pass the word around. Tell the world!'

Men began to pour from the saloon, to mingle with the milling crowd outside.

A blonde-haired girl in riding costume mounted on a white horse came up the hill. She hesitated when she saw the crowd. A puzzled frown wrinkled her brow. She squared her shoulders and rode on.

The outer edges of the crowd broke to let her through. A few men lifted their hats. The girl nodded her head and smiled in acknowledgement of the greetings. She looked very cool and beautiful.

A big Irish miner with a mop of red hair beneath a pillbox cap stood suddenly in her path and looked up into her face and grinned.

'Mornin', miss. Is it out for your constitutional you are while us poor spalpeens sweat an' slave.'

His little piggy eyes meant trouble. The girl urged her horse forward. He stood his ground until the horse was almost on top of him. Then the girl reined in.

'I don't want to run you down,' she said. 'Please let me pass.'

'Here's one o' your fillies from the big houses,' bawled the Irishman. 'A mine-owner's doxie. Let me pass she says or I'll ride you down. That's the way with

128

'em. They treat *us* like filth, but it's them who are filth—'

'Cut it out, Mick,' said a voice from the back of the crowd.

'What lily-livered skunk said that?' bawled Mick. 'He's the sort who'd let people like that,' he flung out a thick arm in the girl's direction, 'walk all over his face.' He thumped his chest and looked up at the white-faced girl. 'But you can't do that to an O'Grady, miss. No-sir!'

'Let me pass, you madman,' said the girl.

'Madman am I? A cheap mine-owner's doxie calls me a madman.'

The girl's face flushed, her blue eyes blazed. She raised the quirt from her side and lashed the Irishman across the face with it. He staggered back, his mouth open, a big hand at his cheek, his eyes wide with stupefaction. This did not last long, however: his eyes fumed wickedly. He cursed and grabbed the horse's bridle. His other hand reached up for the girl.

'Mick,' shouted somebody in the crowd warningly. But others egged the Irishman on.

The girl struck again desperately as the big hand raked the skirts of her riding-dress. O'Grady caught the blow on the temple. He staggered, cursing. Then he righted himself and grabbed again. A shot rang out, the slug whining near over the heads of the crowd. A voice shouted: 'Stand still, you big skunk, or I'll drill you!'

O'Grady's hands fell to his sides. His little eyes were wicked, his face brick-red as he turned slowly. The crowd was parting to let the young Texan through. He had a smoking gun in his hand and murder in his face.

129

He strode to within a few feet of the big Irishman. 'You cowardly skunk,' he said.

O'Grady said: 'You wouldn't say that if you hadn't got your gun.'

The young man's eyes flamed. With a smooth swift co-ordinated motion he sheathed the gun and stepped forward. O'Grady's eyes widened, he threw up his hands. The Texan's fist smashed right through his guard and hit him flush on the mouth. Curses spilled with the blood from his battered lips as he staggered backwards.

The Texan followed him up. His lean dark face was suddenly pale and taut. Something almost maniacal shone there. Still cursing, O'Grady flailed with his beefy fists. One connected with the young man's shoulder, rocking him on his heels. But it did not stop him. One fist smashed again into the Irishman's mouth, making him splutter with pain. Another terrific blow hit his ear with a mushy smacking sound. He teetered, his eyes began to cloud. He staggered into the walls of the crowd.

The Texan followed, his fists driving again and again into the half-unconscious man's face. The young man seemed inhuman, a terrible fighting killing machine.

'Stop it!' screamed a voice. 'Stop it, Hank, please stop it.'

At the sound of his own name the Texan dropped his fists. He stood, looking a little dazed, then he turned and looked up at the girl.

'I'm sorry, Miss Katherine, I guess this man got my goat.'

130

Behind him O'Grady slid away from the crowd, slid slowly forward and toppled over on his face. For a moment the crowd was silent. Then a man nearby shouted: 'He can't do that to our mate.'

'Get him!' shouted somebody else, and others took up the cry.

The young man whirled; once more his gun seemed to leap into his hand.

'I'll drill the first man who tries anythin',' he said.

At the back of the crowd another voice bawled: 'That goes for us too.'

Heads were turned. On the stoop in front of The Venus stood Oakie Jones with a Colt in his hand. Beside him, grinning all over his vacant face, was Shiner – with a shotgun. There was also Gonzales, who favoured a Colt, and last but not least Lawyer Sanderson with his famous silver-plated derringers. His sonorous voice spoke then.

'Shame on men who make war on women.'

Men's feet scraped in the dust. There was a murmur from the crowd. The young Texan suddenly spoke again: 'This young lady is a visitor to Virginia City. Is this the way you treat your visitors? That the person she is staying with happens to be a mine-owner is not her fault. Furthermore, she is a friend of mine.'

'The younker's in the right,' bellowed a man.

'You betcha I'm in the right.'

Over the heads of the crowd Lon made a sign to Shiner. The wide-eyed youth led his pardner's horse forward. Lon mounted.

'Let us through,' he said. The crowd made a lane, and he and the girl rode through it and on up the hill.

131

For a moment neither of them spoke. Then the girl turned and looked at the man and said: 'Thank you, Hank.'

'Forget it,' he said curtly. He did not look at her, but she continued to look at him. She said: 'You're angry with me aren't you – because I did not acknowledge your greeting when the carriage passed you last night.'

'Forget it I said.' His voice was suddenly harsh.

She went on: 'I was angry with you then. We made friends out there the other morning.' She paused, and when she spoke again her voice was little more than a whisper.

'Then you came back into town and killed one of my uncle's men.'

'If I hadn't have killed him he would've killed me. He would have killed me the other night if you hadn't have stopped him.'

'I thought it would end there.'

'If you know anything about the West – and despite the fact that you're now an adopted Easterner, I think you do – you'd know that it couldn't end there.'

'Yes,' she said softly. 'I know that. I should have realized that.' She almost seemed to be talking to herself. 'My father killed a man in a gunfight when I was a child. Although I love the West I hate it too – because of that tradition. You – you're a gunfighter.' Her voice broke.

'Yes. I'm a gunfighter. But I've always given the other fellow an even break.'

'To give a man an even break – that condones everything.' Her voice was bitter.

'You don't understand. You—'

132

'I do understand,' she said wearily. They were climbing steeply, moving among the big houses; the noise of the stamping mills rolling down at them from the mountainside. There was silence between them, which the girl suddenly broke again.

'What were those men doing down there? Something terrible is going on. What has happened?'

He told her the whole tale. He did not mince his words.

When he had finished she said: 'Then my uncle is one of the men you are fighting?'

'I have no quarrel with your uncle. What I had against him was wiped out when I killed Joe Epworth. I am fighting a system. The system that killed Jed and Hanky, and if your uncle is part of that system then I am fighting him.'

'I have learnt a lot in these last few days,' said Katherine. 'I know my uncle is part of that system. I don't like the way he treats his men and the way he and his wife spend the money poor wretches sweat and toil to earn for him. I can even understand and feel sorry for that Irishman who attacked me. He is one of my uncle's men.'

'You accept the fact that I have to fight your uncle?'

She did not answer his question outright. She said: 'You're an idealist.'

'I've never been called that before – but plenty worse.'

'I could call you worse but I won't.' There was no humour in her voice. She reined in her horse. 'I'll leave you here.'

He looked right at her, seeing nothing but honesty in

133

her blue eyes, a little cleft of anxiety in her white fore-head.

'Your uncle has a way out – unless he's too pigheaded or greedy to take it. He can give his men better wages – pronto – and promise them better conditions. If he doesn't do that after the meeting tonight he's only got himself to blame.'

'Yes, I suppose he has.' The girl's eyes became clouded. 'Mebbe I can talk to him,' she said softly. 'Mebbe—'

The man reached out and grasped her hand.

'Katherine—'

'I must go now, Hank,' she said quickly, but she let her hand stay there a second longer before she pulled it away. He watched her go. She turned and waved a gloved hand, and he waved back.

As he rode down the hill his face was grim. But there was a new, happy, yet almost puzzled light in his eyes.

THIRTEEN

By that night the news was all over town. Hiram
Vanberger had delivered his ultimatum to the workers
in his mine. Many of them had gone on strike this
morning. To these he said if they were not back at work
tomorrow they were finished. A bunch of them had
gone to work for Oakie Jones, who paid sky-high rates,
probably more than he could afford at this time.
Vanberger would not pay one cent more – they could
take it or leave it. Trouble-makers would be severely
dealt with, and he offered promotion to anybody who
laid information against them.

He was devilishly clever was Vanberger – and
utterly ruthless.

By dusk no news had come from the camps of Pop
Quail and Cy Carpenter, although both of them had
men on strike. But yet another item of news came from
the Vanberger menage. Two new gunfighters had
arrived. It was rumoured that one of them was the
notorious killer, Rafe Gunther.

Lon Burton was thinking deeply about this last item
of news as he strode along the boardwalk of Main St. It
was too early yet for any night life, and most people

were feeding their faces in the hash-houses.

A buckboard rattled down the street and drew to a halt. A voice called 'Hank', sibilantly, a little harshly. He turned. Lulu Sanclaire got down from the buckboard and came towards him. The cow-faced man whipped up the horses, and they went on up the hill.

'I must talk to you, Hank. It's very important.'

'Spill it.'

'I mustn't be seen talking to you here. We must go somewhere quiet. Where can we go?' She looked around her almost wildly.

The cowboy stood there in the gloom and made no answer. 'I know,' she said. 'I know. There's the little cubby the back of the stables. Hanky used to have it – there's nobody there. Quickly, Hank.'

She caught his arm. He could feel her warm breath on his face, a whiff of perfume. He went with her. The alley beside The Venus was quiet; and the stables too. There would be no horses there tonight until later, when the big shindig started.

'I'm glad to see you again, Hank,' Lulu said. 'I was wondering what had happened to you.'

She came closer to him in the darkness, her body brushing his, her hand tight on his arm. He smelled the scent of her once more, and she was warm and soft. But he did not bend.

'What's the matter with you, Hank?' she said.

'Nothin's the matter with me.'

They reached the stables. The doors were closed. Lulu tried them. 'They're locked,' she said. 'We'll have to go round the back. We can get into the cubby from there. I know a way.'

136

'Can't you tell me what you want to tell me right here? There's nobody around.'

'We don't want to stand here talking, somebody might see us. What I have to say will take a little time. What's the matter, Hank?'

'Nothin's the matter I said.' His voice was harsh as he followed her. 'Keep close to me,' she said.

They turned the corner at the back of the stables, and she turned on him suddenly. Her arms went round him, her mouth sought his hungrily. He held her soft body tightly, and he knew everything was wrong. He knew she was bad, bad like Virginia City and casting that same spell over him. With a sudden force of will he pushed her away from him.

'Hank, please. I—' There was something in her voice he could not understand, it ended on a broken, almost piteous note.

From out of the darkness another voice came, a high, cracked man's voice.

'All right, that's enough, that's enough.'

Lon whirled, reached for his gun. A man staggered out of the darkness and fell in front of him. From another point came the sounds of a scuffle, two soft thuds. Gun in hand the young man peered and waited.

The girl went past him and dropped on her knees beside the man on the ground. A sob escaped her.

'What's the matter, Lulu?' said a voice. 'Somep'n go wrong?'

Oakie Jones loomed up out of the darkness, then Gonzales and another man whom the Texan did not recognize.

'There were three of 'em waitin' to jump yuh,' said

Oakie. 'God job I did as I said an' tagged along behind yuh.'

The girl rose in the darkness. She looked in Hank's direction and started to say something, but the words strangled in her throat. He felt pity for her. She was low, as low as Virginia City – lower! And the pity of it was that she herself knew how low she was.

'Get goin',' he said, and his voice was brittle. 'Get goin' – quickly.'

She turned. Oakie started forward. 'Let her go,' said Lon harshly.

The big man halted. The girl did not look back. They watched her until she vanished into the darkness. Gonzales and the other man had vanished too. They reappeared, dragging two men by their heels. 'They'll sleep for a while,' said the stranger. 'Hank – this is Pete Leighton, my new foreman,' said Oakie.

The two men shook hands. 'Glad to have you with us, Pete,' said Lon.

'Glad to be with you.'

An exclamation broke from Oakie as he bent over the nearest fallen man.

'It's ol' Pop Quail himself,' he said. 'He certainly must hate you plenty.'

He rolled the old man over and looked at him closely. His scrutiny was long. Gonzales went down beside him.

Oakie said: 'The old mossy-horn's daid. An' I on'y tapped him.'

'Most likely the shock just stopped his heart,' said Gonzales. 'He was a very old man.'

At eight-thirty the street in front of The Venus Bar was packed with men, a waving sea of heads and a murmur rising from them like surf breaking on a rocky shore or the humming approach of a 'Norther' across the Western plains.

The waves of men lapped onto the boardwalk except for a small cleared space where stood the young Texan, Hank, Gonzales, Pete Leighton and Lawyer Sanderson, who had come along to see that things were done right and proper but was leaning against the saloon window with his eyes closed as if he was asleep.

They were waiting for Oakie Jones, and the crowd were getting a little restless. The lights from the saloon windows streamed out upon them, on their white tossing garish faces, a mouth opening here and there as a man shouted. From posts the other side of the street somebody had hung three hurricane lanterns. All around the doors of shops and cabins were open, and the occupants stood on their front stoops. Pools of light spilled out into the cart-rutted street.

Lon Burton's face was worried. He craned his neck to look over the heads of the crowd. Finally he saw a familiar face coming nearer.

'All right, folks,' he yelled, his face clearing. 'Pin your ears back, you-all.'

Oakie Jones thudded onto the boardwalk. He was panting and sweating a little.

'I've been looking for that pesky kid, Shiner,' he said. 'He's on a horse-stealin' round agin.'

'I know nothin' about it this time,' put in Gonzales quickly.

Oakie grinned. 'I hadda stop the kid. The way things

139

are now he's liable to get his haid blown off. The way he's goin' around gawpin' into people's faces agin too.'

'Did you find him?'

'Yeh, he's comin'. Here he is.'

Shiner elbowed his way through the crowd. His eyes glinted horribly in the light. As he walked his head turned from side to side as he looked at the faces around, as if fearful to miss any one of them. A few times he paused and peered until an insulted growl sent him on his way. Finally he joined the party on the boardwalk and walked quietly to the back.

The meeting began.

There were sullen murmurs from the crowd and a few threats when they learned that there was no more news from the Vanberger camp. The little coxcombe, Hiram, was sticking to his ultimatum, and his mansion up the hill was like a fortress, ringed by armed guards.

News of the death of old Pop Quail was met by a mingled reception. There was no grief. All Pop's miners were worried about was who was to pay them now – and how much?

There was still no news from the Carpenter menage, though the big house where Carpenter lived with his woman, Blanche Delacroix, was silent, and there was no sign of gunmen around it.

'They're probably lyin' low inside,' yelled somebody, 'waitin' to fill us with buckshot if we try anythin'.'

There was a half-mirthful roar at this sally. In all the shouting there was a menacing undertone. It looked like things were still at a deadlock – and the frustrated men were becoming dangerous. They were like hounds straining at a leash: it only wanted a string of hot-blooded words from one of the leaders to start them off.

But the leaders knew what they were doing: they did not speak those words. Instead they began to talk about new rates of pay. The men earned double what they were getting. There were conditions too. New conditions would have to be laid down. The mines would have to be made safer to work in. There were too many accidents and useless deaths. The Texan, Hank, introduced Oakie Jones's new foreman, Pete Leighton.

Pete told them he had worked in silver mines a long time, and there was not much he didn't know about them. Most of them knew him; he had worked for that rat Hiram Vanberger before he changed over to Oakie Jones's bonanza. It was small yet, but it was up-and-coming. Conditions were good, and Mr Jones paid the best rates. Most of them knew what he paid: did they think these rates were good?

Nearly everybody was of the opinion that they were.

Mr Jones is opening out, said Pete, but he can't take all of you. What Pete suggested was that the rates Mr Jones paid should be laid down as those for all miners. The men should demand these rates and refuse to work for anything less.

'There'll always be blacklegs,' shouted somebody.

Pete shook his fist in reply. He was tall and stringy, and his face was pitted with scars from flying chips. 'Rake 'em out then,' he bawled. 'Run 'em out of Washoe. That's the only way to deal with blacklegs.'

A roar greeted these words, and the crowd began to mill like a herd of restive steers. There was a scuffle in the middle somewhere. A man yelled out in pain.

141

Seemed like folks were blackleg hunting already.

Pete Leighton looked a little sheepish. Oakie Jones strode to the front of the boardwalk, and his powerful voice boomed out: 'Hold it, will yuh! What's the matter with yuh, are yuh all goin' crazy?'

His words caused a lull, but there was still a lot of scuffling going on. Worse might have happened had not another diversion occurred.

A closed carriage, handsomely painted in black and gold and drawn by two magnificent greys, came rolling down the street.

The crowd was silent, a sea of turning heads, shining eyes and open mouths. Then somebody shouted: 'It's Cy Carpenter.'

The coach came on. Those at the edge of the crowd opened out to let it through. Then they closed in on it. When it got opposite The Venus Bar it was surrounded by a yelling mob. The yelling died to a hum as the door suddenly opened.

'What's he want?' yelled somebody.

But it was not Cy Carpenter who appeared on the step: it was his wife Blanche Delacroix.

She was a big woman, a perfectly-made handsome woman. The lights gave an added sheen to her long black hair and dark eyes, her ripe lips and bold plump features. She was richly, flamboyantly dressed. This was the way most of the watchers liked to see their women. They were struck momentarily dumb.

Her voice was ringing, a little husky, a little harsh.

'If you will let us through my husband has something to say that will be of interest to all of you.'

'We've heard his speeches before,' growled somebody.

142

'Down the mine with the water dripping down our necks.'

'Let 'em through,' yelled Pete Leighton, the bit between his teeth once more. 'It won't hurt us to hear what he's got to say.'

'Pete's right, let 'em through!' yelled somebody else.

Others took up the cry. Men backed from Blanche Delacroix as she descended from the carriage. The crowd opened out to form a lane up to the front of The Venus.

Cy Carpenter followed his wife down the step, but he turned and held out his arm. A white-gloved hand came out of the carriage and rested on his arm. Then the golden-haired girl got down.

She preceded her uncle up the lane. She wore a long soft brown wrap and a tiny concertina-like hat with feathers on it atop the sweeping gold of her hair, which shimmered like molten sunlight in the bright air.

As she walked behind the bold swaying Blanche, she was straight and slim like a boy. The contrast was striking. She smiled as she mounted onto the boardwalk.

Lon Burton went to her side. 'You shouldn't be here.'

'I should,' she said. 'I had a hand in this.'

He knew what she meant then, and he wanted to grab hold of her and kiss her, to clasp her hand. Right now he dare not do either.

'Speak your piece, Mr Carpenter,' said Oakie Jones. Carpenter stood on the edge of the boardwalk. The light shone on his florid face, heavy jowls and black walrus moustache. He jerked the lapels of his faultless black broadcloth coat. This man who had treated men like dogs and cattle seemed a little ill at ease.

The crowd began to rumble again. Their patience was wearing thin.

143

'Give the man a chance,' bawled Oakie Jones. As the echoes of his voice died away and comparative silence ensued, Cy Carpenter spoke shortly.

'I want all my men back on the job tomorrow morning. No action will be taken, and I intend to pay everyone higher rates.'

A chorus of shouts followed this; a few cheered; many began to yell terms.

Oakie Jones took Carpenter aside. The two men spoke earnestly. Carpenter kept shaking his head. Pete Leighton joined them, and Blanche Delacroix. While this pow-wow was going on Lon Burton and Katherine Dale stood still, looking at each other while Gonzales looked on with his little twinkling black eyes, and Shiner grinned at all and sundry. Lawyer Sanderson leaned on the window like a man asleep on his feet.

The crowd milled and squabbled. The shouting became louder. It died to a rumble as Oakie Jones stepped to the edge of the boardwalk and raised his hand. The big man shouted:

'Mr Carpenter has agreed to pay the rates fixed, the same rates I am paying in my mine – he has also agreed to do something about working conditions as soon as possible.'

A roar greeted this pronouncement. Pete Leighton pushed Carpenter to the fore again. He was scowling, but as he stood there he looked at his wife, and she smiled. His face lightened a little then, and he bowed. He gave his arm to his wife, the other to his neice. She threw a triumphant glance back at Lon Burton. They went down the steps and the lane opened to let them through once more. They got into the carriage. As it rumbled away a large section of the mercurial crowd began to cheer.

FOURTEEN

The meeting was over. Many folks went about their business, but even so The Venus Bar was packed almost to suffocation. The fortunate miners were celebrating their victory. Others, belonging to the Quail or Vanberger menage – and particularly those of the latter – were still in a state of uncertainty and unrest.

A bunch of them, still vociferating, milled around the bar where stood Oakie, and Lon Burton, and Pete Leighton. Another group nearby was composed of Gonzales, Lawyer Sanderson and Shiner, who had so many people around him that his head was on a perpetual swivel as he looked into faces. By his side the lanky lawyer was guzzling unashamedly and beaming once more on his flock.

'We cain't do nothin',' Oakie Jones was saying. 'All we gotta do is wait till the morning an' see what happens. You fellers keep away from the mine – I'll find jobs for as many as I can – Vanberger cain't work his bonanza with no men.'

146

RED SILVER!

A shouting man burst through the door of the saloon. His words were communicated along. Others took up his cry, one by one, became silent. The message reached those by the bar. By that time the talk in the saloon had died to a mere hum.

The notorious Rafe Gunther, Vanberger's new hired killer, was coming down the street. He was looking for the man Hank Blundell.

All eyes were turned on the lean young Texan at the bar.

'There was another man with him,' said the one who had brought the news.

The Texan did not say anything. He was staring into nothingness, his eyes dark, his face bleak. He looked as if he had already assumed the cold-blooded gunman's almost trance-like state. Nobody in the saloon could guess what his thoughts may be.

The sadness and frustration that was filling him did not show in his face. That night, not so very long ago, in the face of a beautiful woman he had seen a glimpse of heaven. He had known hope, but now that hope was gone. He felt like a man being forced into a black pit of hell . . . .

Then all feeling left him. His brain became ice-cold, and there was not a tremor in his hands. He made that little loosening shrug of his shoulders; he curled and uncurled his fingers. He was unbeatable – and he was damned. People moved away from him.

'Hank—' said Oakie Jones. Then he stopped as he saw the look in the young man's eyes.

People were crammed into the corners, back against the walls. A wide lane opened between the doors and

147

that section of the bar where the Texan stood alone. There was only one hope in his mind: *that* the crowd could not know either.

A man looked through the window and hissed suddenly. Bootheels thudded on the boardwalk outside. Then slowly the doors opened.

A thin stoop-shouldered man came in. He was dressed in a shirt, pants and vest of a rusty hue. He might have been young, he might have been old; there was something ageless about his narrow white face which had the appearance of scraped and polished bone. The only live thing about him was his eyes. They held a steady, bleak glow.

As he crossed the threshold his hands, white and crooked, a little like talons, swung gently to and fro below the tied-down holstered guns on each thigh.

Another man came behind him. A tall heavy catlike man with almost Indian-like colouring and features, cruel and with eyes like black coals. His thin lips were curled in a sneer and he had one hand hooked into his belt, the other motionless at his side.

The first man spoke in a high, perfectly toneless voice.

'I'm Rafe Gunther. Where's that lily-livered skunk who calls himself Hank Blundell?' He looked around him and his dark-featured pard moved away from behind him, his black eyes raking the crowd on both sides.

Gunther's eyes seemed to have flitted across the lone figure against the bar without seeing him. The young man took a couple of steps forward and said: 'Hank Blundell's right here, Gunther.'

148

The man's bleak eyes focused then. There was no surprise in them as they looked at the young man, but they changed; they almost seemed to soften a little.

The stoop-shouldered man, his arms dangling, took a few more catlike steps forward. Then he did a surprising thing: he hastened his steps and thrust out a hand.

'I don't hafta fight you, Burton,' he said.

The young man came forward, his own hand outstretched. The two of them met in the middle of the floor and clasped hands.

From behind Gunther came a cry of rage, a blasphemous curse.

Gunther whirled, the crowd scattered. Then from in their midst an anguished cry rang out.

'White Fox ! White Fox!'

Almost simultaneous with it a shot rang out.

The gun of Gunther's Indian-like pard was half out of its holster. He tried to get it further, but his limbs would not obey his command. His other hand clutched at his chest, and through his clawed fingers blood began to seep. He crumpled slowly and fell on his side.

The boy Shiner ran from the crowd. There was a smoking gun in his hand. His lidless eyes shone with a newer, more terrible light. He went down on his knees and peered into the agony-etched dead face.

His words came clearly, a whisper that mesmerised the crowd into silence.

'White Fox! White Fox, the renegade, who killed my maw, an' my paw, and my sister.'

Shiner began to sob then, great gasping strangled sobs which shook his frail body, the heart-tearing sobs

149

of a man who at last understood.

Oakie Jones crossed the floor and helped the boy to his feet, led him back to the bar. Then pandemonium broke loose as men surged forward.

Oakie Jones was standing beside the lean young Texan, his arm around Shiner's heaving shoulders. The big man said quietly: 'He called you Burton. It wouldn't be Lon Burton would it?'

'Yes. It would. I'm sorry, Oakie, I—'

'Forget it. I understand. Your reputation came before you. I had an idea—' He paused. He shrugged. 'Lon Burton, Hank Blundell – it's all the same to me.' The huge hand squeezed the young man's arm.

Lon broke away and dived into the press that was cutting Rafe Gunther away from the rest of them. The notorious gunman – as notorious even as Lon Burton – was shouting as the young Texan reached him.

'Listen, everybody! I've something to say!'

Gradually the babble died. In his queer high toneless voice Gunther said:

'The man who calls himself Hiram Vanberger sent for me a couple of days ago. He hired me to fight a man called Hank Blundell. At that time I did not know who Hank Blundell really was. I think Vanberger knew. But he didn't tell: he's full of tricks like that. Maybe he thought I would not hesitate to kill a friend for money. That is the way he is made.' Gunther lowered his head a little. 'I have done many things in my life, but I still have my creed.' His voice rose again. 'Lon Burton saved my worthless life once; I'd sooner die for him than try to take his life from him.'

Rafe Gunther had nothing more to say. After his

words had finished there was almost dead silence for a moment. Then pandemonium broke loose again, more furious, more savage than ever. Men surged towards the door. The body of White Fox was trampled beneath their feet. They spilled out into the street in tumbling waves. One name was on their lips; one terrible purpose.

Lon Burton, shouting, started away from the bar. 'Stop them!' he said.

He dived into the back of the crowd and was almost knocked from his feet by men who hardly saw him now. Oakie Jones caught up with him, grabbed his arm and dragged him free.

'There's nothin' you can do now.'

'There are gunmen—'

'Most of the crowd have guns too. And there are hundreds of 'em.'

The bar-room was almost empty. The body on the floor looked like a tattered, red-painted doll.

A sonorous cynical voice said: 'At least we can be in at the death.'

Lawyer Sanderson tottered away from the bar, took a few prancing steps then fell flat on his face.

'He ain't goin' no place,' said Oakie Jones. 'Leave him there to sleep it off.'

The rest of them followed Lon and the big man to the door.

The street outside was almost empty, the yelling savage mass of humanity was already surging up the hill. Slower, milling.

'They're there,' yelled Lon Burton.

Almost simultaneous with his words came the shots.

A scattered few at first and then a crackling barrage, spreading and becoming clearer as many in the crowd began to retaliate.

'*Madre de Dios*,' said the panting Gonzales. 'This terrible night will be remembered.'

As the party got nearer the crowd were moving again. The picket fence was down, and they were attacking the door and the windows of the huge gimcrack house.

'They're gettin' away,' yelled somebody. 'Goddam 'em. Stop 'em!'

Men were fleeing through the grounds of the house. One threw up his hands, a grotesquely twisted silhouette, then crumpled to nothingness in the shadows. Waving lanterns tossed light among the sea of the crowd.

Fleeing men were pursued. Some were brought down, but many were allowed to get away as the pursuers returned to the house.

A screaming wide-eyed negro was tossed from hand to hand over the crowd. He was engulfed then spewed forth. He rolled in the dust, rose and ran limping away.

Windows were smashed and the front doors were smashed inwards and trampled upon. A mighty roar went up from the crowd as another man was tossed above their heads. A ragged little man whose eyes bulged with terror, whose mouth yammered with screams that none heard. He was engulfed, and the crowd surged forward with him in their midst. They surged around the side of the house, out into the open in an ever-spreading mass.

Lon Burton was running ahead of his party as he

reached the edge of the crowd. He began to fight his way through. He was buffetted from side to side, twice he was thrown back.

The crowd surged and then came to a waving halt. The primeval roar which had seemed to be part of them, to be issuing from the bowels of some huge blood-lusting beast, died a little. The greater press of people surged around a gaunt tree, and from the midst of them came the screams of the doomed man.

A rope snaked through the air and fell over an out-thrust bough, the ominous loop etched for a moment. The crowd roared again and then above their heads a screaming man suddenly swung. The screams died, and the man who had called himself Hiram Vanberger kicked for a moment then became still.

Pressed in amongst them so that he could not move Lon Burton felt the shudder go through the ranks as the murmuring slowly died. Then the ranks broke, the mob became separate people again. Lon Burton was left alone.

He looked upwards a little longer. 'I didn't want it to finish like this, Mike,' he said. Then he turned away.

AFTERMATH

The big door opened before the young man could raise his hand to the knocker. Blanche Delacrois stood there. She smiled and moved away as the young man entered. Then she turned and went up the stairs at the side.

A girl with honey-gold hair ran down the hallway to meet him.

'Katherine,' he said and caught hold of her.

She laughed. 'Don't be impatient,' she said. 'First of all there is somebody I would like you to meet.' She caught hold of his hand and pulled him along.

She opened a door and ushered him into a room. A tall grey-haired old man with seamed kindly features stood there.

'Lon,' said the girl. 'I want you to meet my father.'

The two men, both a little awkward in the presence of the girl it seemed, gripped hands. Then the girl went.

The old man stood straddle-legged. 'Sit down, son,' he said.

'Thank you, suh. I'd rather stand.'

The old man smiled. 'So would I,' he said. 'I never

155

could get the hang o' sitting on the edge of a chair an' drinking little cups o' tea. It's a new craze yuh know – comes from Boston they tell me.'

Lon did not say anything. He had an idea the old man had not finished. He was right.

The old man said: 'I'm a plain-spoken galoot. I've got something to tell yuh so I'll out with it without any more smart palaver. I came to fetch Katherine because I'm leaving Milwaukee an' goin' to Oregon to start another ranch. It's wild country, but it'll be a new rich land when it's tamed – strangely enough the women seem to be all for it.' He paused. Then he went on:

'There's just one more little thing. I've kinda got outa touch while I've been livin' with the hoi-poloi. I want a good foreman – a young man with plenty of drive – to help me get goin' once more. Will you take the job?'

The young man seemed to flinch a little. 'I'm Lon Burton,' he said.

'I know all about you, son. What's good enough for my daughter is good enough for me. Whatever you've been I know you've also been a damn' good cowhand. C'mon, yuh young skunk, git off'n that one leg, what d'yuh say?'

'What do I say' echoed Lon Burton. He grinned and stuck out his hand.

The old man took it and wrung it heartily. 'Katherine,' he boomed.

The girl came into the room so quickly it was evident she had been leaning on the door.

'He's all yours,' said her father as he passed her.

It may have been an accident that the old man left

the door slightly open. But it was no accident that he leaned on the jamb and inclined his ear towards the crack.

He heard Lon Burton say: 'I'll marry you – but there are certain conditions—'

'Conditions is it? You'd better be careful or I'll say "no". What are these conditions?'

'I want Oakie Jones to be best man. An' there's a few guests – Gonzales, an' Lawyer Sanderson, an' Pete Leighton, an' Shiner.' The young man's voice was suddenly louder. 'Katherine! Shiner's all right! – we'll make a man of him. It's like a miracle!'

'I know,' said the girl softly. 'Dad's already got a job lined up for Shiner.'

The man's voice was a whisper as he spoke her name. Then there was silence, and with a smile the old man outside moved softly away from the door.